# NOW IT'S DARK

# Now It's Dark

*by*

Lynda E. Rucker

Swan River Press
Dublin, Ireland
MMXXIV

*Now It's Dark*
by Lynda E. Rucker

Published by
Swan River Press
at Æon House
Dublin, Ireland
June MMXXIV

www.swanriverpress.ie
brian@swanriverpress.ie

Cover design by Meggan Kehrli
from artwork by John Coulthart

Set in Garamond by Steve J. Shaw

With thanks to Paul Barnes for his support.

Paperback Edition
ISBN 978-1-78380-780-2

Swan River Press published
a limited hardback edition of
*Now It's Dark* in January 2023.

# Contents

❦

# Introduction

I think sometimes we get trained to think that short stories are like fireworks. They blaze across the sky, make some sparkly impression, perhaps a loud bang, and then they fizzle out in an instant. We're supposed to ooh and ahh, and then discard the memory of them, and wait for the next one. Lynda E. Rucker's stories are not fireworks. They are strange, murky, brooding pieces of doubt and introspective tension—and they don't explode across the night sky, they *are* the night sky. And they don't try to make you jump with a big bang—they're never as merciful as that. What's that you hear? It's a rumble. It's a growing rumble, ominous and growing in pressure in your head, and it starts as you begin to read and it lasts long, long after the story is over. Why won't it go away?

Let's state the obvious first. *Now It's Dark* is not a novel. It is, indeed, nothing remotely like a novel. But I do urge you to read it as a novel, because I think that in its growing momentum from story to story is where its curious power lies. Lynda E. Rucker's weird and precise fictions aren't merely individual, they are cumulative. These stories were written over a number of years and for different publications, and the fact that they are gathered together is our good fortune rather than the result of some overarching plan—they're clearly intended to work in isolation. But it's the very particular nature of Lynda's very particular take on horror that invites you to see each story as a sly commentary on one you've already read. They become not merely a series of shocking tales, but one longer narrative in which themes of dissonance and disassociation bleed into each other. The overall effect is mesmerising. *Now It's Dark* can be a bunch of fireworks if you like—truth be told, Lynda can set off fireworks as well as anyone I know—but to me it reads like an essay on how the uncanny works: not only within fiction, but more pertinently, within the cracks of our own lives.

The contract short stories make with the reader is that there is some puzzle to decode. We read on, so we can learn the rules of the story, and how to interpret the plot and the characters. We wait to be rewarded with an ending where everything becomes clear—perhaps with a nicely surprising twist as a pay-off. The lie of these stories is that there is a single obvious truth to discover at all; that stories are little puzzles to solve. It's a reassuring way to look at fiction—the idea that there is a particular way the writer wants us to think or feel, some inevitable conclusive message we are supposed to take. Lynda E. Rucker has no interest in giving us any such bogus reassurances. You go into any of her stories with a heightened sense of awareness—you feel that anything she draws your attention to in passing might have some sinister significance, might be the clue that'll help you find a truth you can't quite discern. But I don't think Lynda believes in simple, objective truths—her stories are instead maps of possibilities. She knows that, just like her characters, you are struggling your way through her twisted plots—and so, cheerfully, helpfully, she's there to offer suggestions along the way. Take the first story in the book, "The Dying Season", in which a woman tries to grasp at the unease she feels in a subtly sinister leisure park. As soon as you think that the strange couple our heroine encounters are murderers out of a home invasion movie—once you suspect that the food she's eating might be binding her forever to a dreamscape like a Greek myth—Lynda has her characters articulate these very ideas. As soon as they're spoken aloud, they sound banal and unconvincing; always, the characters laugh. By highlighting the clichés of horror, Lynda also closes off the possibility of their use. So as you try to decipher Lynda's worlds, she seems to be there at your side, gleefully yanking away all the easy answers that make you feel secure. There's nothing more reassuring than a ghost story when you *know* it is a ghost story. The brilliance of a Lynda E. Rucker story is that you emerge never quite sure whether it was a ghost story or not—you just know it was more disquieting than a simple explanation can allow, and the truth underpinning that story's world is far larger than the few thousand words the tale can encompass.

Why, after all, would Lynda E. Rucker want to reassure us? Her characters never get to be reassured—why should we be? They live in constant doubt, right to the precipice of insanity. She invites us, for a brief few pages, to join them there upon that precipice. Which leads me to the most back-handed of compliments: I'm always relieved when I reach the end of a Lynda story. I never quite realise how tense one makes me feel until I've managed to escape.

And why? There's no writer I know better at creating liminal space—that region of unknowing and unliving. Of *unbelonging*, I think, in a way—from this American writer who has these last few years lived in Germany and Ireland and Britain, inhabiting each of them in turn but refusing to take on their identity. She takes that empty liminal, and she populates it with characters yearning for something—anything—they can't begin to articulate. For substance. The ghostlands in Lynda's stories aren't just places that people visit—they're a summation of who these people are, their frail, contradictory selves. Most stories put their characters into a state of crisis—that's how drama works. Lynda's characters are the crisis, and they come to realise that they've been screaming their rage and despair for a very long time. The reality that we perceive doesn't add up—and that reality is beneath the skin.

Liminality is never merely of place, but of emotion. People falling out of love with each other not *because* of something, but of a vague and intangible sense that life is askew. When I read these stories I become convinced that this is the absolute truth of things: that our lives are rarely destroyed by some soap operatic drama, but because we're beaten down by the creeping knowledge that somehow, somewhere, somewhen, things got bad. We take wrong turnings we never recognise and stray into a liminal space we can't find our way out of again.

It's what gives Lynda's work such weight. For all its chill, it is never cold. The danger of horror is it reduces people to objects. What is so bruising about the stories in *Now It's Dark* is how nakedly emotional they are. Or rather, how so nakedly they are crying out for emotion, for some empathetic connection—reaching out for some sort of love, some sort of passion, some sort of *point*. There is an existential flavour to a Lynda E. Rucker tale, but it never submits to it, it is never prepared to concede to a universe too harsh to comprehend.

Maybe the problem is we try to comprehend at all. I always get the sense that Lynda resists attempts to analyse her worlds too closely. In "The Séance", our narrator is obsessed with the work of a dead painter she grew up with as a child: the story tries to square the memories of the schoolgirl with the dark reclusive misanthrope her friend will become. It's that collision between raw and terrifying Art, and some safe rationalisation of it: Lynda simply doesn't want to be rationalised for your comfort, thank you very much. To be defanged—to be made safe. In "The Unknown Chambers", a woman subordinates her life to the rediscovery of a forgotten writer of horror and philosophy—the more she becomes enthralled to the subject, the more she loses herself. To trace autobiographical explanations upon an artist's work is to reduce them. The Lynda E. Rucker I know as a friend is silly and giggly and endlessly funny. The Lynda E. Rucker I know as a writer is dark and looming and uncontainable. She writes that, "We have never taken women at their word. Always, always, there must be something deeper driving them . . . Women can never be whole; they are only good to us if they are damaged." Come on, Lynda seems to tell us. Here is a story where sense is broken. Here is a pain that cannot express itself. Are you so arrogant to think you can fix it? Diagnose me, if you dare.

What makes Lynda's stories profound to me is the way they never seek our approval. We're privileged to witness her labyrinths of dream and nightmare—we aren't invited to solve them. The very first paragraph of this book uses the word "unbeautiful"—I think that's the key. The world of Rucker is so distorted that it's impossible to perceive quite where horror bleeds into cathartic release, where beauty becomes unbeauty. In "The Other Side", a man is haunted by a dream in which he finds severed hands of children sticking out of the mud—he'd been looking for something beautiful, and found this. And then, as the dream moves on, the hands become the beauty he was seeking. In "The Secret Words", a woman discovers notes she made about a childhood game she played with her sister. She reads about this game of the stone and the sky and the moss, and how her sister began crying, "even though we were just getting to the good part". There is no clue what the game might be; the adult cannot remember. In that unknowing, the game becomes at once something wondrous and something terrifyingly horrific. The longer you spend in Lynda E. Rucker's thrall, the more that reality bends out of shape, and the more you begin to appreciate its awful beauty and its tortured comforts, like some twisted Stockholm Syndrome.

Perhaps my favourite story of the book is the last one. "The Seventh Wave" seems to sum up the book as a whole. It is the tale of a woman caught between two boring men, and the inarticulate passion she feels, and the inarticulate passion of the ocean. It's about the cruelty of love, and the cruelty of the absence of love, and the cruelty of the denial of love—and how all of them can be used as a weapon. And it is pure Lynda E. Rucker: funny but numbed, numb and yet bursting with emotion. A harsh world made utterly redemptive.

And within all the thrilling contradictions, I am reminded of this, from the opening to "The Séance", describing the artist at work: "The few extant photographs . . . are unrevealing. They are at angles that almost invariably fail to capture her face . . . When her face does appear . . . it is often at the edge, only a slice of her, the remainder of her body lost beyond the border of the lens." Here, then, is a slice of Lynda E. Rucker. Here is *Now It's Dark*. Take care as you try to find her, hidden beyond the borders of the lens.

Robert Shearman
November 2022

*Now It's Dark*

*For Sean Hogan, finally.*

# The Dying Season

At dawn the leisure resort was still and quiet, prefab cabins and trailers jumbled together and sleeping soundly, and along the harbour all was peaceful. The peace would not last; the unseasonably warm and sunny weather so late in the year as October, and particularly for an English seaside village, meant that soon it would be jammed with dog-walkers and families and couples strolling up and down the concrete seafront, taking in the last of the light and the warmth before winter closed in altogether. It was, on the face of it, an unbeautiful shoreline: massive concrete steps leading in low tide to piles of dead black seaweed washed up between large wooden groynes. But the dawn's high tide meant that now the sea lapped the steps, while the colourful sailboats glistened in their moorings, the rows of pastel bathing huts were washed in the morning sun, and the sky was a skein of impossible blue with strips torn for clouds.

Sylvia headed up and away from the concrete harbour and to the nature trail that ran above the estuary. The horizon opened before her as she jogged along the scrubby grasses. Gulls wheeled overhead and the shore below was a wash of late-season pink thrift and purple sea lavender. The sea beyond sparkled.

The wind was stronger here and whipped her hair in her face. There was just the wind and the sound of her own breath, and that was a good thing, the tension that still clutched her body from the previous night draining out of her. Big

3

gulps of the fresh salt air. She could run forever. She ought to run forever. She could do it, just vanish away; wasn't the seaside magical enough for that? An Anglophilic childhood in America, raised by an English mother, had taught her as much. Viking longships churn across the waters waiting to attack; Jamaica Inn shutters itself to guests and hides its secrets; Merriman Lyon waits by the standing stones, gazing out to sea. There might still be magic here to spirit her away. There might. If only she could run fast enough to catch hold of it.

"Goddammit," John had said the previous night, shoving his plate away. "Why are you bringing *that* up again?" Today, she couldn't even remember what *that* had been.

"I wasn't," she said. "I didn't mean—" but of course, she did mean, or he said she had, so what did any of it matter?

She ran harder. The tears leaked out the corners of her eyes and were lost on the wind. Now the rhythm of her run beat out two phrases. *I'm sorry. I didn't mean to.* Over and over, spoiling the morning, spoiling everything. Just like she always did.

"I'm trying to fix things here," said John's voice in her head. "I'm trying to make it up to you. Why won't you work with me a little bit? Why won't you help me out? *What's wrong with you?*"

She wheeled round, heading back. She wasn't alone on the trail anymore; as she ran, she drew even with and passed a couple. They both had jet-black hair, were thin and slight and poorly dressed for the weather, the girl in a filmy dress with bare arms and her companion in an equally diaphanous shirt and thin trousers. Perhaps, she thought, they were tourists from someplace much warmer, tricked by the brightness of the day. The wind must have felt cutting to them, and she made a grimace of solidarity in their direction as she passed, but they ignored her.

4

Back at the leisure park, all of the cabins and trailers looked the same. John had been coming here with his parents since he was a child, so he knew exactly which one was theirs, but she'd had to memorise the twists and turns on the gravel pathway in order to find her way back, and even so, she found herself standing for a long time deciding between two cabins, unable to identify which was the right one. For a moment she had the mad idea that both were, or that she was choosing a destiny: walk into one, make the right choice, walk into the other, make the wrong one. But then she thought she heard music coming through the window of one, something classical that John listened to a lot, and what sounded like a child's voice drifted from the window of the other.

"You're just in time," John said as she stepped in. He was wearing an apron and piling up food on a plate: bacon, sausages, grilled tomatoes, a fried egg, a mound of toast. Her stomach clenched. She wasn't hungry; she hated a large breakfast anyway. He knew that. But she couldn't say it. She couldn't be difficult. Not now.

"Thought I'd walk up to the harbour in a bit myself," he said with what she told herself was not a forced casualness as she chewed her way methodically through meat, bread, more meat. "I need to check my email and I can't get a signal in here. The signal's better there."

She was glad her mouth was full because it prevented her saying all the things she wanted to say: *That's funny my signal's fine. Why are you really going to the harbour? Who are you phoning? I'll come with you.*

She ate as much as she could but still knew he was going to be angry at her because it wasn't enough. And so despite everything, she was relieved when he pushed his own plate away and said, "Right, back in a bit," and headed out. She dumped what was left on her plate in the trash and washed the dishes, then sat for a while on the sofa listening to her stomach rumble unpleasantly.

A hammering at the door startled her so much that she simply stared through the glass for a moment at the girl on the other side of it. It was the girl from the nature trail. She'd changed into a shapeless hoodie over leggings, and her stringy dark hair framed a pale narrow face. She smiled in a way Sylvia thought was meant to be encouraging and friendly. It reminded her instead of the bared teeth of a monkey.

"I . . . Hi, can I help you?" Sylvia said through the door, which felt standoffish but the girl gave her the creeps.

"We're just in the cabin over there," the girl said, nodding her head in a vague direction, and Sylvia detected what John would call a posh accent, "and we're wondering if you've any milk we can borrow? Just for coffee."

"Oh! Of course!" She still didn't ask the girl in. She opened the door just enough to pass the mug of milk through, keeping the glass between them, then felt a rush of guilt for being so unfriendly and added, "My name's Sylvia. I think I saw you up on the nature trail? Do you spend a lot of time here?"

But the girl was already turning away, saying something about family friends of her boyfriend. Sylvia watched her walk away up the gravel path but couldn't see what cabin she went into.

She'd had time to shower and do her make-up by the time John returned. She resisted the urge to ask him something leading like "Anything good in your email?", but she couldn't help saying, "Something weird happened while you were gone."

"Oh?" He was only half-listening, had picked up the remote and was flicking through a series of unpromising-looking programmes.

"This girl came by to borrow some milk, but something about her bothered me."

"Bothered you?" He finally looked over at her. "Did you say someone was bothering you?"

"No, I just mean there was something off about her I couldn't put my finger on. She said she and her boyfriend were staying somewhere over that way"—waving her hand as vaguely as the girl had—"and that the place belonged to some family friends of her boyfriend, or something. But you know what I kept thinking? About those horror movies, you know, like the home invasion ones?" John loved horror movies, the more violent and gory the better. Sylvia hated them but watched them with him to appease him. "The ones where they go in and kill all the people and then act like they're the ones who live in the house? I kept thinking the girl reminded me of one of those people."

John kept channel surfing. After a moment he said distractedly, "That's a bit mad."

She said, "I know. I mean, I didn't really think it. It's just what it reminded me of. She seemed weird."

John threw down the remote. "Fuck all on the telly as usual. I'm going to do some work and then let's walk into the village. Get out a little bit."

"Yes," she said. "That's where we went wrong yesterday. Too much time sitting around here getting on each others' nerves."

John said, "What are you talking about? Yesterday was fine." Then he was gone, out of the room, and she heard the shower come on. While she waited for him, she went out on the porch to see if she could see the girl again, or anyone else, but there were no signs of life at the leisure resort at all. Even the child who'd been shouting from the nearby window had fallen silent. They might have been all alone there.

❀

John often worked remotely from his London office and it allowed them the leisure to take off midweek from the city occasionally just as they'd done this time. Sylvia lay in the bedroom and tried to read while he worked, but she couldn't seem to focus on either of the books she'd brought.

She dozed off. The next thing she knew John was shaking her awake and saying they ought to take that walk. As they wandered into the village and round a few indifferent shops she couldn't get over the feeling that she was still dreaming. There wasn't much to do in town, and she said they ought to pop into the Tesco and pick up something for dinner and head back, but John suggested they stop off at a pub. It was nice enough to sit outside even though the sun was setting. A group of men had commandeered the bar inside, but they were alone in the grassy garden.

"Funny listening to the conversations in there," she said. "The one man was bragging, saying his missus had her own money and he had his and they went out with their friends as they liked when they liked and it wasn't like before with Yvonne."

"It's just local people talking."

"I know," she said. "I didn't mean anything—"

He said, "I know it's not as witty and sophisticated as the things your artist friends talk about, but then maybe if you paid a little more attention to what people are really like you'd sell something."

Once she would have bitten back at him in self-defence, but she had long since learned that such an exchange would be futile. Something passed between them. She thought, *I'm going to leave him*. She wasn't sure yet, when, or how, but in that moment she knew it in her bones, and the knowledge was as irrevocable as knowing you had terminal cancer or that it was raining outside or that you were another year older. As soon as she thought it, it became immutable truth.

8

He said, "Shall we have another?" like nothing was wrong, and she agreed. She could do this, she could play this agreeable part as long as she needed to. It was almost liberating, like being somebody else entirely. Send the real Sylvia away for a time and let some acquiescent creature take her place. Then behind her she heard someone say, "Oh, look, it's our neighbours," and she turned and it was the couple again. The girl was wearing an unsuitable dress again, this time a thin white one far too insubstantial for the chill edging in along with the dark. She had combed her dark hair and made up her pale face so that it was even paler save for the dark smudge of her eyes and ruby lips. The two of them looked like a pair of vaguely out-of-date and out-of-place goths.

The girl said, "I'm Lynne and this is Gabriel. Mind if we join you?" Of course they minded, but what on earth was there to say? And then Gabriel bought a round, so they were trapped. Still, Lynne and John appeared to be hitting it off, and John rarely hit it off with anyone. Sylvia leaned forward to Gabriel, who seemed always on the verge of smiling contemptuously at a joke only he was in on, and said, "Lynne was saying something about your cabin belonging to family friends—"

Lynne and John stopped the conversation they were having and fell silent; Gabriel shrugged and said, "People Lynne's parents know," and Lynne turned that bared-tooth grin on her and nodded. "Just some people," she said. "People we know."

"I was asking," Sylvia said, "because John's been coming here since he was a little boy and it's my first time and I keep getting lost. Do you have that problem? I guess at least if you walk into someone's house around here they're not likely to shoot you like they might in America."

Gabriel said, "Well, there are a lot of hunters and fishermen around here. Our cabin's full of books about it.

And trophies." Was that the hint of a foreign accent she detected? She couldn't tell. Anyway, they could go now, they'd had their pints, but John wouldn't hear of leaving, he had to get the next round, and the evening passed into a haze just like that, two more pints turning into four more pints turning into who knew how many. Lynne said she was a clothing designer and Gabriel was—what was Gabriel? At first Sylvia thought it was something to do with new media, some kind of managing editor for a music publication online, but later there was something about his recording studio, so she wasn't sure. She thought their circles in London must overlap someplace, but when she threw out a handful of likely names they both shook their heads, looking bemused, smiles playing at the corners of their mouths. She was drunk. Why was she trying to make sense of anything?

Then it was last orders and she was laughing and leaning on John and the stars reeled overhead and it was just like things used to be and what had she been so upset about anyway? They should eat something, the four of them, and a Chinese takeaway across the street was still open. They ordered spring rolls and chicken with oyster sauce and chips and staggered back down through the town. John was walking ahead with Lynne and she was lagging behind with Gabriel, but she couldn't think of anything to say to him and then the sea was off to their left and she could hear it, sighing softly, washing up against the shore. She wanted to run away from the three of them and toward the water. She imagined it, black and cold and endless under the night sky, unpierced by the sliver of moon high above. Secretive. Safe.

"Aren't you cold?" she called to Lynne up ahead of her, but Lynne didn't seem to hear her, and Gabriel said, "She's just like that, she doesn't feel the cold. She doesn't feel many things, really."

"That's a really odd thing to say," Sylvia said, feeling suddenly much more sober. They turned right into the leisure park, into the maze, and Lynne and Gabriel made noises about inviting them over for a nightcap but John said no, he had a conference call early in the morning. She followed John to their cabin but she couldn't shake the feeling he was leading them back to the wrong one. He went right at a point where she was sure he should have gone left. As he fumbled for the keys, she could see the living room through the glass sliding door just as they'd left it. It looked the same, but something was off about it, she was sure of it, something just outside her conscious memory: a piece of furniture moved a foot this way, carpet a nearly imperceptibly different shade. Of course that was silly. Even if she'd been correct about turning left, this place was such a maze that there was probably more than one way to get back to where you'd come from.

Inside, they set the takeaway on the counter and John kissed her hard and then he was pushing up her skirt and pushing aside her underwear and shoving himself inside her, there in the kitchen with the counter hard against her back. She gasped and lifted her head and that was when she saw Lynne, from the window over the sink, standing some yards away but staring at them, her pale face ghostly in the dark. Sylvia cried out and shoved him away, and he stumbled back, and it would have been comical if he weren't so angry, but now there was no Lynne to be seen out there. Of course there was not. "What the hell?" John said, and she said, "I'm sorry. I thought I saw someone."

"Don't be stupid," he said, and she said, "I know, I'm sorry," but she'd set off another argument as usual, and the next thing she knew she was waking stiff and sore and tangled in bed sheets. Her head was pounding and for a few awful moments she could not remember where she was. The previous evening was nearly a blank: she could remember arguing, and trying to apologise—her, not John—and then not much after. She went into the kitchen for a drink of water; the plastic bag of Chinese food was still sitting there on the counter, untouched.

A run might clear her head. She went out into a bright cold morning. The wind whipping across the sea had an icy quality to it, more so than the day before. It felt like an abrupt shift in the weather and the season, just as something had shifted in her the previous day. Across the water black storm clouds gathered.

As she ran past the harbour to the nature trail the wind intensified, biting at her face, tearing the moisture from her eyes. It was too much. She turned, cutting the run short.

Back in the leisure village, she tried to retrace their steps from the previous night, turning right where John had when she thought he should have turned left. She ended up in front of a cabin that looked like theirs, but it couldn't be; the way hadn't circled round, it had gone off in the opposite direction, and so she went back the way she'd come. This time she went right. Once again, the cabin looked the same, but now she must have been mistaken, there was something taped to the glass of the front door and there hadn't been before. No, she couldn't be wrong; she had followed this path every morning for the last three after her run.

The thing taped to their door was a note, written in an angry scrawl.

*We could hear you last night, everybody could all around with your sex noises, and it was disgusting, this is a family place and we are here with our families not like you filthy people and your fucking. What are we supposed to tell our children.*

Sylvia stood stunned, frozen, awash in a stew of emotions: shame, humiliation, fury, despair. She looked all around, as though whoever had delivered the note might still be lurking nearby. The cabins all appeared deserted as ever. She went over to the one where she thought she'd heard the child's voice from the window the previous day. Curtains were drawn across the glass door so she could not see inside, and she knocked tentatively. What she would say when someone answered she had no idea, but there was no response. She peeked through a window, which was uncurtained, and jumped back, startled.

The place was a tip; it appeared to have been ransacked, clothing and other items strewn across the floor, plates of rotting food stacked about. It looked as though no one had been in there for a long time.

It also looked much the same as their own cabin, from what she could tell under all the mess: roughly the same furniture layout, the same furniture even. Maybe all the cabins came furnished the same way and people didn't bother to change them around.

Sylvia stumbled back. She ran back to their cabin and burst through the door calling, "John!" only to be confronted by a thunderous look; he was on the phone. Of course, the conference call. He made go-away gestures to her like she was an unruly pet. She dropped the note on the carpet and fled into the shower, fled him, fled everything. She turned on the water as hot as she could stand and scrubbed till her skin was raw and it still wasn't enough. Then John was hammering at the door. She cried, "Hang on!" but he shoved it open anyway, shouting, "What the hell is this?" and when she peeked round the shower curtain he was waving the note at her like it was her fault.

She shut the water off and grabbed her towel, winding it round. "It was on the door. Someone had taped it to the door when I came back from my run. And John, I think there's something wrong in the cabin beside us—"

"What the hell? Who the hell did this?" John rubbed his hand over his face. "How am I supposed to—I know the

13

people here. They know my family. They've known me since I was a child. What am I supposed to do? How am I going to face them?"

She was aghast. "How are they going to face you, more like—John, that note's insane. Who would do something like that? What's wrong with people?"

She didn't want to add that she couldn't remember the previous night at all, after the argument in the kitchen; had they gone straight to bed? Had they been loud? Had they been so loud that people in other cabins could hear them? Her memory was a featureless blank, undisturbed even by fitful dreams.

John slammed the bathroom door, shaking the entire cabin. She waited there for several minutes and then crept out. She scurried across the hall to the bedroom, where she shut the door, dressed quickly, and began shoving things in her bag, her mind racing. She did not want to spend one more moment in his presence. She could push the bag out the window, stroll past John in the living room and say she was going for a walk, circle round and grab her things, walk into town, bus, train, home, back to their flat before he'd worked out she was truly gone as opposed to vanishing in a sulk for a few hours. She could then get anything important she needed and stay with a friend while she figured out what to do next.

She was still throwing things into her bag when John came in the room. "What are you doing?" he said. "Why are you packing? We're not going to be driven out of here by anyone. We have just as much right to be here as anyone else." She said, "I'm just trying to get organised," but his questions deflated her. She thought of what it would take to run away from him, to leave him. Her head hurt and her body was exhausted and she just wanted to curl up and sleep for a very long time. She said, "Anyway, we need to get back to London soon," and he said, "What for? Some dilettante friend of yours smearing herself with mud and writhing around on stage again?"

"Sarah's not a dilettante," she said, "and anyway it wasn't mud it was—never mind." She shoved the bag off the bed. There were better ways to leave him, better ways to make that plan once they'd returned to London. At the moment she needed sleep. The hangover she'd hoped to clear out with the run had taken hold with a vengeance. She crawled into bed and slipped almost immediately into a dream in which she was running along the shoreline, only instead of bathing huts it was lined with the leisure park's cabins and trailers. All of them had fallen into disrepair. Some had had their fronts torn off and the furniture inside was rotting and falling through floorboards. She kept thinking she just needed to get past them and up to the nature trail but she seemed to be running in circles, or they were just endless, and something was pacing her, just at her heels, though when she turned her head she couldn't see anything. Then whatever the thing was grabbed her and started shaking her roughly, and John's voice said, "Wake up. We've got a dinner invitation from Lynne and Gabriel," and she swam groggily to the surface. Had she really slept the entire day away? She was starving, and realised she hadn't eaten anything since the unwelcome breakfast the previous morning.

She crawled back out of bed and ran a comb through her hair. She looked terrible, puffy and worn. She was making herself a cup of tea in the kitchen when John came in and said they were already running late and had to go. "Five minutes," she pleaded. "What, do we have a booking they're going to give away if we aren't punctual enough?" But he kicked up such a fuss that in the end she left her tea there cooling in its mug and followed him out.

She said, "How do you know which one is theirs anyway? I can barely find ours," and he said, "They told me, they stopped by while you were sleeping." She supposed that if you knew the leisure village well enough certain things must serve as landmarks, but as far as she could tell they were just walking in circles past the same cabins. John came up in front of one that was exactly like all of the others and said in a satisfied voice, "Here we are!"

"Welcome!" Lynne said, opening the door to them, and as they went inside Sylvia felt vaguely disappointed by how ordinary this cabin was too. Table, chairs, a couple of sofas, a television, a gas fire flickering warmly and a kitchenette off the one side.

She said, "It looks almost exactly like ours."

"Oh, yes, they're all the same," Lynne said vaguely, but there were some differences. Gabriel had mentioned hunting but not taxidermy, though it too was clearly a hobby of the owner as evidenced by several somewhat worn-looking birds—she identified a pheasant, a mallard—mounted on solid bases on the mantel. A shelf near the fireplace held books on the topic along with manuals about angling and hunting.

"Hope you like curry," Gabriel said from the kitchen, and they all agreed that yes, they liked curry, and Lynne brought them wine and they sat on the sofa and Sylvia drank the first glass much too fast, but afterward felt calmer. Lynne poured her a second and she sat back. The room was warm and the curry smelled so good and maybe John was right. Maybe she needed to relax. Maybe things were in her head. Maybe she was the problem after all.

She was lost in thought and paying no attention to the conversation around her—this was another thing that drove John mad—when she realised John was reading something. It was the note that had been taped to their door.

She said, "John, don't!" but it was too late, and no one was paying attention to her anyway. Her face flamed at hearing the words spoken, and remembering the shock she'd felt on first seeing it, but the other three did not seem to share her sense of humiliation and outrage, least of all John who'd been so angry in front of her. Lynne turned toward her while they were all still laughing and it occurred to her that what bothered her about Lynne's smile was that all of her teeth were too small. They looked like two tiny, even rows of baby teeth in an adult mouth, an adult face.

She murmured, "Sorry, where's your bathroom?" even though she knew based on the identical layout of their own cabin, but they didn't hear her anyway, so she got up and slipped into the hallway and tried the first door, the one that was the main bathroom in their cabin. It appeared to be locked. Out of curiosity she tried another door, one she knew must lead to a bedroom, and it was locked as well. She stood indecisively for a moment or two in the hallway until their laughter reached her again, and then she tried the third door. She knew from the layout of their own place that it would be a bedroom with a half bath just off of it.

This door opened, and the light switch illuminated a plain room that appeared unused. Just a bed, a bureau and no personal items. There was a shelf above the bed with more books on it about hunting, and mounted on the wall, above that, dominating the room, the pale skull of something with enormous antlers. It must have been a stag, she thought, with its hollow eyes and jagged opening that she guessed must be the snout, the nasal cavity, but which looked like a shrieking mouth.

Imagine how restful a night you'd have with *that* over your head. In the bathroom, she washed her face and hands and looked at herself in the mirror for a long time. She didn't recognise the face that looked back; her eyes looked as hollow as those of the poor dead stag. The wine and heat had flushed her cheeks but it was an unhealthy, feverish flush.

She shouldn't drink any more, certainly not before eating something.

She deliberately did not look in the direction of the skull again, and back in the living room no one seemed to have even noticed she'd left. Gabriel was dishing up dinner at last, heaps of basmati rice and rich yellow curry, and she fell on it ravenously.

"Easy," John said to her, "it's not going anywhere," and she stopped, embarrassed. Gabriel tried to smooth it over by saying, "It's nice when someone appreciates your cooking," but that only made her feel more self-conscious. Lynne, poking in a desultory way at her plate with one fork and twirling a wine glass with her other hand, said, "You must not look at goblin men, you must not buy their fruit."

Sylvia said, "What?"

"It's from the Rossetti poem," Gabriel said. "You know, you aren't supposed to eat fairy food or you'll be trapped with them forever. Lynne and I were working on a project a while ago based around it."

"I hope this doesn't mean we're stuck here at the leisure park for the rest of our days," Sylvia said, and they all laughed. It must have been too much wine on an empty stomach that made her add, "You know, I had the funniest thought when I first saw Lynne. That you two didn't belong here. That you'd done something with the people who really lived here and just made yourselves at home."

As soon as it was out she regretted it, but they were laughing again, thank goodness they all laughed, and Gabriel said, "Not sure you'd have to kill anyone to move into one of the cabins this time of year, it's all pretty easy pickings," and they all laughed more. She joined them though she didn't even know why.

"That reminds me," she said. "One of the trailers near us, I think someone might have broken into it actually. It looks like it was ransacked or something. Is there some kind of security here?"

"The Liddells," said Lynne, and nodded solemnly. "There was some trouble there, actually."

Gabriel nodded. "The father. He went a bit mad—it was awful, the police came and everything. They took him away."

"That surprises me," John said. "I've known the Liddells for years. I'd never imagine something like that from them."

"Well, you know," Lynne said solemnly. "They say you just can't tell with families."

They all sat silently for an appropriate moment or two contemplating the sad fate of the Liddells, and Sylvia said, "What about these people, John?"

"What about them?"

"You know just about everyone around here—do you know Gabriel and Lynne's friends, who this cabin belongs to?"

John looked blank for a moment, then shook his head. "It's a big place. A lot of people are transient. I don't know everyone, just the regulars right around my family's cabin."

"You weren't kidding about the enthusiastic hunting," Sylvia said. "That's quite a trophy, the stag back there," and she inclined her head in the direction of the rest of the cabin.

"Oh, yes, that," Lynne said.

"It's kind of creepy," Sylvia said, and John said, "A stag?" and Lynne said, "You should see it, John. Come on back, I'll show it to you."

Sylvia and Gabriel sat in silence after they had gone. Finally Gabriel broke it by asking if she wanted more curry and she said no, she'd had enough, and they continued to sit there.

"Taking their time," she said with a nervous laugh, "it's not that much to look at," and, "I'm going to see what they're up to" and Gabriel said, "I really wouldn't if I were you."

"What do you mean by that?" It felt like the first honest thing she'd said to anyone in days.

"It makes you look clingy and suspicious," Gabriel said. "I don't think John would like that. I know Lynne wouldn't."

She thought then of all the things she ought to say. Things prefaced by arch remarks like *I beg your pardon* or even a properly inflected *Excuse me*? She did not say anything. She and Gabriel sat there and waited and they looked at each other, and she thought how small and strange he was, imagined his pale face a mask to hide a hideous creature beneath it.

Gabriel said, "What do you think they're doing back there anyway? It's not what you think."

"How do you know what I think?" she said, but even as the words were out she felt like she knew his answer, that he knew exactly what she thought, that he knew everything about her, and John too, that they both did and had since their encounter on the nature trail the previous morning. That she ought never to have looked upon them in the first place, or given them something of hers and John's—the mug, the milk—or eaten their goblin fruit. As soon as John came back they would leave. She would make sure of it. Even if she had to make a scene, a terrible embarrassing scene no one would ever forgive her for, and what did she care what any of the other three thought about her anyway?

She said, "I hate this time of year. Everything coming to an end. It depresses me."

"I guess it all depends on how you look at things."

"What other way is there?"

He shrugged. She guessed that he wasn't really in the mood for conversation.

An unsettling chill had settled over the cabin despite the merrily burning gas fire. Any moment now John would emerge with Lynne and she would insist that they go home.

Not just back to the cabin, but home-home, all the way back to London; there was still time to catch the last bus and the last train if they were quick about it. Or—she could just leave.

"I feel sick," she said, and set her wine glass down. "I have to go. Tell John I'll see him back at the cabin." She was entirely done with social niceties, and without another word she stepped out the door into a night so black and cold that it momentarily seized her breath. The moon sliver from the previous night had been swallowed up by clouds and she was forced to make her way nearly blind. She knew she was on the path because she felt its gravel under her feet, but then there was grass, so now she must be wandering between cabins. Then she no longer cared about finding her way back to the cabin at all, only out of the leisure park. If she could get to the main road, and the harbour, and into town, she had her purse with her and she could buy a ticket or even thumb a lift if it came to that.

She dug her phone from her pocket so she could use its light, but the battery icon was red and draining fast. On impulse she thumbed John's number, but his phone simply rang and rang and his voice told her to leave a message or send a text if it was urgent. Then the screen went black. She could hear the sea nearby, and she moved toward the sound with the certainty that if she could get near enough to the sea, she would be safe, but the sound, or her ears, deceived her, shifting, now behind her, now before her.

When the clouds above parted at last, the feeble light of the faraway moon revealed that she was at the edge of the leisure park. The cabins behind her waited, and across the black strip of road the sea would be surging against the concrete steps of the harbour. She had the idea that she had emerged into some kind of purgatory, that she might wander an eternity among the empty cabins, but then a car's oncoming lights loomed up ahead and she stepped to the roadside and put out her thumb. To her surprise, the car came to a stop. A worried-looking middle-aged woman popped her head out of the window. "You lost, love?" she asked. Sylvia said, "I don't know, I need to get to the train station," and the woman said she was on her way to Colchester and would that do? Sylvia said yes, of course it would.

As they sped away she imagined John might have gone to look for her by now, might have discovered she was not back at the cabin. She felt she owed the woman some explanation, so she said, "Thank you. I had a fight with my partner. I just want to go home now and talk it over with him later," and the woman said, "You don't need to explain, love, these things happen." Sylvia pulled out her dead phone again and looked at it, wishing she could ring John and make sure he was okay. The woman commented that it was very late in the year and hadn't the leisure park shut down for the winter? Sylvia found she could not answer her. She could not speak again at all except to thank the woman who drove her right up to the station, where she bought a ticket with minutes to spare. She ran down the platform to her train, dodging other travellers and their piles of luggage, but she could not shake the feeling that she was no longer real, that if she touched anyone she would vanish like the mist rising off the pavement. She leapt aboard her train and was still making her way down the aisle as it eased out of the station.

Then the lights of the station were behind them, and the sound of the engine was the sound of the sea, and they were gliding into a night that was dark, and secret, and uncharted.

## The Séance

The few extant photographs of Anthea Wainwright are unrevealing. They are at angles that almost invariably fail to capture her face. Most of them are snapshots that happened to catch the back of her head, or she is a distant figure in some shot where someone or something else is the subject. When her face does appear in photos, it is often at the edge, only a slice of her, the remainder of her body lost beyond the borders of the lens. According to her nephew, she loathed cameras; not out of vanity as is the case for many of us, but from an unshakeable conviction that there was something fundamentally unnatural about the way they preserve a likeness of a moment in time that might otherwise have gone unnoticed. Not the occasion itself, but the juncture; the split second the shutter clicks, the way the atoms and molecules align themselves in the milliseconds that bring the photo into being. Such slivers of moments are not meant to be recorded in such a manner, she maintained. She behaved, the nephew said, almost as though she genuinely believed the camera was capable of robbing her of her soul.

These were, of course, a child's observations, filtered now through an adult's perceptions, and at least a decade and a half old. But they are insightful. Until the last two years of her life—during which she communicated with virtually no one—Anthea had been close to her older sister's son in that way that adults and children who feel misunderstood by or out of step with their peers can sometimes be. He admitted that the loss of her when he was twelve had been devastating, something he perhaps had never rightly recovered from.

But how Anthea would have loathed the modern barrage of relentless self-chronicling, the endless preservation and exhibition of every moment in text *and* photographs. It was, Justine observed dryly, almost as though she'd died because she saw the twenty-first century barrelling down on her and found it too horrific to contemplate. Perhaps she had perished the moment before the clock struck midnight on 1 January 2001. A new year; a new decade; a new century; a new millennium; on the edge of a brave new horror of a world, perhaps Anthea Wainwright had simply willed her heart to stop beating, had exhaled one final breath from her lungs and refused to draw another.

Of course, there was no way of knowing, because Anthea Wainwright had already become, at only thirty years of age, a full-fledged recluse, and by the time her body was finally discovered after neighbours, in a depressingly clichéd coda to her life, complained about the smell from her New York apartment, it was impossible to determine with any accuracy when the death had occurred. We know she was alive at some point on the day of 30 December because that is the date on the postmark and check she mailed to the landlord that covered six months' rent—unfortunate as this surely delayed the discovery of her body. After 30 December 2000, we have no evidence that she was in contact with anyone or even alive.

It was said that three of the emergency personnel who found the body took leave and never returned to their positions. If any reasons were stated, they were kept confidential, but on the face of it, it was unlikely to have been due to the circumstances of Anthea Wainwright's life and death because, tragic and gruesome as it might have been, her seclusion and early passing was no more tragic and considerably less gruesome than the injuries and accidents that the EMTs would have encountered on a regular basis. Everyone agreed she had been an off-putting woman, but it was difficult to imagine that off-putting nature had been transferred to her decaying corpse—no more so, that is, than the reasonable degree of off-puttingness any decaying corpse might inspire. Maybe, Justine suggested, it was the hoarding, but I do not think that can account for it, and neither, really, does Justine.

It is one more mystery we are attempting to solve in our quest to chronicle the art and short life of Anthea Wainwright, the artist, the poet, the scholar, the eccentric, the prematurely dead, and not in the beautiful pre-Raphaelite way that young women are supposed to be prematurely dead. No, she must have been a stew of fluids and rotting flesh by the time they found her. I say this to Justine. She makes a face and says she doesn't want to think about it. I can't stop thinking about it. I go online and Google for photos and descriptions of bodies found in similar circumstances. I think of Anthea Wainwright swollen and blackened and leaking everywhere.

I reread the nephew's email. "I lost her when I was twelve as well," I say, not to him, not to anyone but myself. The nephew had asked me how I first learned of Anthea Wainwright, what had piqued my interest in someone so obscure, not even a blip on the art world's radar. Like others, he sensed something personal in my quest. And of course there is. Anthea was my dearest girlhood friend: my confidante, my first love, my nemesis, all the things that girl friendships are made of. Then she moved away, and I never saw her again.

The first time I saw Anthea, I thought she was a ghost. She was so pale, with white-blonde hair shining in the sun, and she was dressed all in white. She was standing on the edge of my backyard, which abutted the parking lot of the old sanctuary of the First Baptist Church. We were ten years old.

I was walking out the back door, taking out the trash on my mother's orders, and I was so startled when I saw her that I dropped the trash bag. She ran over to me then and said two words: "Hide me."

I said, "*What?*"

She glanced back over her shoulder. "Hurry," she said. "I ran away. They'll be looking for me as soon as they find out." I was trying to figure out what she was wearing. It was something like a bathrobe, but not quite. She flapped her arms then to show annoyance at the garb. "They were going to baptise me, but I ran away."

My next response was, "*Why?*" I am not even sure what I was whying, the baptism, the flight, or both.

"Because," she said, "it's all stupid. I don't believe in any of that stuff. Jesus and all that. I hate it."

I was shocked. My family was not particularly religious, but my mother dutifully sent me off to vacation Bible school every summer, and this *was* Georgia in the 1980s. You didn't go around saying things like you didn't believe in Jesus. I mean, I had heard of people doing so, but I never imagined myself face to face with someone who did.

I made a split-second decision. "Come in," I said, and held the back door open for her. She sprinted across the lawn and into my house. I could hear my mother vacuuming in the living room and I grabbed Anthea by the hand and dragged her into my room. "We're about the same size, you can borrow some of my clothes," I said. I was giddy with the spirit of adventure that had seized me with the appearance of this strange and unpredictable new friend. I pulled some shorts and a t-shirt out of a drawer and was shocked when Anthea unzipped her robe and dropped it at her feet to stand there naked. I had grown increasingly private and self-conscious about my body over the last few years—as I thought of it, I wasn't a little kid any more—but Anthea didn't seem to have a scrap of modesty about her. She pulled on my clothes and we just stood there looking at each other.

"Well," I said, because you had to say something.

"Thanks," Anthea said. She picked up the baptismal robe and rolled it under one arm. "I'll get these clothes back to you."

"How?"

"Well," Anthea pointed out in that *well-duh* voice she would often take with me over the next two years, "I know where you live."

"Are you going to get into trouble?"

She shrugged. "Probably. But at least I won't be baptised!" She grinned, and her face lit up. I hadn't thought she was pretty until that moment.

I said, "Whose class are you in at school? I don't remember you."

"I go to the Christian school," she said, and I went, "Ohhh." The so-called Christian school was a dubious educational enterprise with a student body of just a hundred or so. Everyone in town knew that the school's real main purpose was to allow white people to keep their kids from sharing classes with black kids.

"I hate it," she said. "My parents make me go there. It's stupid. School is stupid. Church is stupid. Most things are stupid. Not you, though."

I felt gratified at being pronounced not a stupid thing by this girl. After just a few minutes' acquaintance, I was certain she was everything I wanted to be and was not. Fearless, disobedient, irreverent.

"Anyway," she said, "I'll see you later," and she walked out of my room and I wondered if that was the last I would ever see of her.

A week later, I was lying in bed reading when I heard something scrabbling at my window screen. Before I had time to be afraid, a girl's voice said, "Hey! It's me, from the other day."

I crawled out of bed and went to the window. "What are you doing?"

"Talking to you at the window." *Well-duh.* "Let me in."

"I can't," I said. "My mother will hear me. It's late."

"Okay," she said. "Listen, there's a bush out here, so I'll leave your clothes under it and you can get them in the morning."

I felt that little thrill again. It was all so clandestine, like we were spies or solving mysteries or something. "Did you get in trouble?" I asked her.

She shrugged. "Some," she said. "What's your name? I'm Anthea." I said I was Gail, and she said she had a sister named Gail but she was all grown up, and I said I didn't have any sisters or brothers either. And then, as abruptly as she'd turned up, she announced, "I'll come back over soon in the daytime. I'll see you later." That was what she always said, whenever we parted.

I found my clothes under the bush in the morning, just as she'd said. Two days later she came over in a normal fashion, knocked on our front door and talked to my mother like a regular little girl and not a spy or someone on the run, and from that point on, and for the next two years, we were inseparable. From the minute our respective schools were out, we were together, though rarely at her house—her parents were older, and very strict; they were the kind of adults I thought of as "mean parents", and seemed to disapprove of children on general principle. Even at that age, it seemed obvious to me that Anthea had been an unplanned and unwanted addition to the family. They'd tried to deal with it by making as many rules as possible in the hopes she would be as little trouble as possible. Unfortunately for them—and maybe because of all the rules, who knows—Anthea was many things, but "little trouble" was not one of them.

We spent most of our time at my house, or running around the neighbourhood playing. Anthea also insisted that we regularly set aside a time she called the Art Hour. The hour bit was subject to interpretation; in my recollections, at least, the Art Hour sometimes dragged on for many hours. But Anthea said she was going to be an artist when she grew up, and so it was vital she take this time to improve on her skills.

Even outside of the Art Hour, she was always doodling in one of her little sketchpads. We'd be sitting outside talking, and all the while she'd have a pen or pencil and be busily scratching away and then she'd show me what she had drawn. Sometimes it would be a sketch of me, but more often she'd have drawn something inanimate in our vicinity. Even then, Anthea would take an object like a tree and render it into something that was simultaneously more fantastical and more real. The tree would *look* less like the tree I was gazing at, but it would *feel* more like it. Anthea had a gift for grasping the innate qualities of a thing, so if it was a sinister tree or a kindly tree or a tree with secrets, you somehow knew that after looking at one of Anthea's drawings even if you hadn't realised it when you looked at the tree itself.

"How do you do that?" I asked her once, and she said, "Do what?"

"That doesn't look like the tree." I pointed at her sketch pad. "Only it *does*. It looks more like the tree than—than the tree does!"

Anthea looked at her drawing for a few moments, and then back at the tree. "But that *is* what it looks like," she said at last, her face blank and guileless.

We fought, too, viciously, as kids do, and she could be merciless when she was angry. Sometimes I hated her. She was prettier and smarter and more talented than me. She was better in every way, and we both knew it.

Although I would like to say otherwise, everything was changing by the time she moved away. I don't think we would have remained close had her family stayed in the area. I was developing a deep crush on her that I couldn't or didn't want to name or understand—wasn't I supposed to feel that way about boys, not girls?—and she was increasingly impatient with and bored by me. She was moving on, and I was not.

The last sight I had of her, she was standing in her driveway near the Mayflower moving van that would take all their possessions to Florida where her father's job was transferring them. Like always, she said, "I'll see you later." She was stoic and I was sobbing; she pressed something into my hand and I did not realise until their car was off down the road and out of sight what it was: one of her sketchbooks.

I opened it and flipped through the pages. I'd never sat and looked through one of her sketchbooks from start to finish before—she'd never allowed it—but here it was, like a diary of our time together. Two or three of my own face, those trees with all their peculiar personalities captured, a neighbourhood cat, the old Baptist sanctuary, my mother's hands as she sliced a cucumber.

For such a long time, my memories and that sketchpad were all I had of her. We exchanged a few desultory letters after her departure, but they tapered off quickly, and then she was utterly gone from my life for three decades.

*Thought this might appeal to you*, said an email I received a year ago from a colleague, with a notice attached of a small gallery showing in Decatur, just outside of Atlanta. The name caught my eye before I looked at the images: surely not? Not the most common name, but at the same time, there was no doubt more than one Anthea Wainwright out in the world. The colleague had no knowledge of my childhood best friend; he had simply surmised from the style of her work that the exhibition might appeal to me.

And it *was* the work that drew me initially, not some misplaced childhood loyalty or leftover adolescent torch-carrying, but the images created by the woman I'd never known, images accompanied by sparse lines of poetry with the style and thematic concerns of a modern-day and more macabre Emily Dickinson, intimations of pain and death.

If Anthea loathed exposure in photographs, the opposite was true when it came to paintings. She was the central subject of nearly every one, and in those paintings, she made herself more raw and vulnerable than photographs ever could. She mostly painted herself naked, and her self-portraits relentlessly chronicled the indignity of the human body inextricably entwined with a ferocious female sexuality. You could almost smell the sweat and the blood, taste the tears and saliva. She gave these paintings provocative names to drive home her intentions: *Orgasm* and *Discharge* and *Vulva*. The thing is, most of the paintings aren't explicit, but they feel like they are. You feel like a voyeur looking at them because you know that she is using her body to lay bare her soul.

I sometimes imagine that sex with her must have been like that as well; that there would not, could not, be anything casual for Anthea in the meeting of bodies. She'd have been equally intense in everything that she did. Justine and I have not been able to find much in the way of personal relationships in her life, though, of any nature. She had been an intense child and a loner save for our friendship; that seemed consistent with what I have learned of her later years as well. I can imagine her being entirely celibate.

I sense that Justine is jealous of Anthea. I don't ask her, of course, and of course, on the face of it, it makes no sense. It was Anthea, after all, who brought us together. Justine was the first person at that Decatur gallery that the nephew contacted. I need her expertise; my specialty is literature, not art. Medieval hagiographies, to be very precise, although I spend more time than I'd like trying to get undergraduates excited about *Beowulf*.

But Justine is the type of woman who wants her lover to be consumed with her, and she knows that I am only consumed with Anthea. Photos of her paintings—yes, I get the irony—cover my walls, not just my workplace but throughout the house. The scraps of her writing that survive are strewn about the kitchen table. I have bits of Anthea everywhere, because I am trying to make connections, I am trying to understand what she was telling us with her work, and I feel that the more I immerse myself in her world, the more likely it is to come to me.

Because Justine loves me, and I am not obsessed with her, she opts for the next best thing: she tries to share in my obsession, like a woman befriending the mistress of her unfaithful husband. It is as though the ghost of Anthea is always with us, lurking in the corners or up near the ceiling like the strange entities that inhabit her paintings. Watching us from the margins. Lying between us at night while we sleep. I feel her breath on us when we make love.

I have always found the notion of academics as disinterested scholars to be an absurd one. There is a school of thought that says we are supposed to be unconcerned with notions like "quality" or whether or not we *like* something; it is this disinterestedness that allegedly allows us to be superior cultural critics, that imbues us with the ability to analyse a car commercial with the same seriousness that we might bring to Chaucer.

I labour under the unpopular-in-my-circles belief that in order to be an expert on a particular piece of art or body of work, you *must* love it. Love inspires empathy, and we need empathy to approach and understand art. We academics protect ourselves with enough jargon and neuroses as it is. It's silly to pretend we are scientists setting out to create objective experiments around art. Even the hardest of hard sciences have their biases; the analysis of art is nothing *but* bias. I tell my students this; I say that I am letting them in on a secret and breaking the rules. And I am unafraid to love Anthea's paintings.

Yet I find it difficult to choose a favourite among them. They can be divided into two sets: those in which she is masked and those in which she is not. The masks she chooses vary; some are beautiful, ornate Venetian-style half-masks—Columbinas, Justine tells me they are called—but most are grotesque. Several are of the terrifying beaked medieval plague mask variety while others are animal heads. One is a horse skull, and Anthea's eyes are staring out from the empty sockets, blazing with despair. Justine ventured to wonder how Anthea got the skull on her head until I reminded her that these are paintings, fabulations. Justine laughed and was embarrassed and tried to brush it off, but the fact is that these paintings feel like a truer representation of Anthea than the handful of photographs her nephew sent us.

Then there is the other set of paintings, those in which she is not masked. In these she has manipulated her facial features. In one painting she is screaming, but her lower jaw is elongated and monstrous; in another, she has covered her flesh in bleeding pustules; a third has her reaching into her throat and tearing out what appears to be handfuls of ropy muscles.

I like these less than the animal mask ones only because they are painful to look at, that she is driven to maim and disfigure herself in this way. I feel as though it is not right that she should be so exposed; I want to drop a cover over them and hide her from the world.

And then there are the other things that are with her in all of these paintings. I call them the homunculi. Some are more monsters than women or men—covered in hair, or bearing the face of a dog or a monkey, or with scales in place of flesh. The ones that do resemble men are grotesque: in a number of the paintings, they sport disproportionately enormous erect penises as large as they are. The women are less overtly sexual but more animalistic; they have the watchful looks of something studying its prey, or their faces are twisted in cruel parodies of ecstasy.

These homunculi are found all along the borders of her paintings, as if they are making their way from the edges of things into her world. In every painting she is in a room, generally the same room, one that looks like an attic with wooden floors and a pitched roof. Maybe it is her apartment, but unlike the descriptions I have heard of that place, crammed from floor to ceiling with boxes and jars and papers, this room is bare save for the occasional piece of furniture acting as a prop such as the wooden chair that Anthea is sprawling in or bending over. The homunculi often leer at her from the ceiling; sometimes they are passing into the room from the walls behind her and other times they are foregrounded. For the works that can be dated, there is a progression in her awareness and distress; over time, her attention is drawn more to them and her anguish comes more directly from their presence. In the ones with the latest dates on them, she is looking directly at them. It is as though she has given up on beseeching her audience. She knows that she is all alone with these creatures she has made.

On Anthea's death, the estate had gone first to her older sister, the other Gail, as their parents had passed away a few years earlier, and shortly after to the nephew while he was still a teenager as Gail was diagnosed with late-stage breast cancer and died in a matter of months. Before that happened, though, the landlord needed Anthea's apartment made habitable again, and the nephew remembered his mother complaining about having to pay companies that specialised in hoarders and cleaning up crime scenes. Nearly everything not immediately identifiable as one of Anthea's paintings was discarded, so we have little to go on—if she kept notes or journals, they have long since rotted in some landfill.

As for what Anthea lived on, particularly in those final years—however unknown she was to the wider art world, there is evidence that she had a few wealthy private clients. This suggests there is existing work by her out there in the wider world, but thus far, all of our enquiries have turned up dead ends. The paintings remaining in the apartment were shipped to Atlanta and placed in storage, and there they sat for nearly fifteen years until the nephew contacted the Decatur gallery last summer about a showing.

I asked him what had prompted him to do such a thing after so long, and he simply said it seemed like it was time. I cannot fault his cooperation, although by no means are we getting something for nothing: Justine is still cataloguing Anthea's work and preparing the paintings for further exhibitions. The nephew is an insurance man, a head full of statistics and life expectancies and not an artistic bone in his body, but he loved his aunt and wants to do right by her legacy.

In the last year or two of her life, she had cut even him off. He has given us all the letters she wrote him prior to that point, and they are charming documents, full of whimsical drawings and imaginary stories about ordinary days running errands round New York City where store clerks are badgers and public transit is via elephant and camel, and post offices are staffed by various species of birds that fly letters and packages to faraway places. Those had ceased abruptly, and although he wrote her a number of times after that, she never replied.

Her final relationships were with a handful of gallery owners who were interested in her work. Those soured in the end as well. They all said she was wildly unpredictable, even by the standards of those accustomed to dealing with the erratic and temperamental. She would demand certain parameters before agreeing to an exhibit and then repeatedly failed to follow through. As she became increasingly abusive and refused to deliver, they abandoned her. The picture they painted was of a woman who was almost feral. She was rank; she wore filthy clothing and she smelled; she was irrational, spoke nonsense half the time, was as unpleasant in behaviour as she was in appearance.

We have names, convenient categories of disease for people who suffered as Anthea suffered. Bipolar. Borderline personality disorder. Schizophrenia. At first I did believe her to be mentally ill in some way.

The more I learn about her life and her work, though, the more I realise how erroneous that initial armchair diagnosis was. Now, new words dance in my head to explain Anthea's art and life.

Haunted. Influenced. Possessed.

Can you catch evil spirits the same way that you catch a cold? It's not entirely random, after all, who catches a cold and who doesn't when everyone is exposed to the same virus. Catching it requires a certain systemic vulnerability, a lowering of bodily defences.

If you were the type of person who was able to see beyond things—if you were an unusually sensitive soul, prone to grasping the faintest of nuance, and the very essence of things . . .

But there is something wrong with this story. A colleague to whom I showed some of Anthea's work seized upon a diagnosis of childhood sexual abuse, but I am not so sure. Perhaps I am merely overly resistant to the psychoanalytic school of criticism, but there seems something needlessly, even dangerously reductionist in this theory.

The same thing happens to my medieval saints; in modern hands, these powerful women become broken ones: abused, anorexic, mad. We do not take them at their word. We have never taken women at their word. Always, always, there must be something deeper driving them as we locate their savage imaginations in origin points of trauma. Women can never be whole; they are only good to us if they are damaged.

My Anthea is undamaged, undiminished, not receiver or receptacle but creator—yet even the creator can come to regret her creations, to be menaced by them. Even God saw his beloved morning star, Lucifer, betray him.

There is a story I have been keeping to hand, an old story from the pulp era about a painter whose grotesque work obsessed his audience and drove them mad; the story spirals to a fever pitch in which the discovery is made that the painter worked not from his imagination but from actual photographs. I have not shared this with anyone, because what am I to say about it without sounding as mad as we claim Anthea must have been?

And we arrive at last at this night. It is very late—one or two or three a.m., I do not know because the times on my laptop and my phone do not match and are clearly wrong and the only real clock in the house, above the kitchen table, has stopped—and I have been brewing pot after pot of coffee and gulping it down until I am half-mad; as Balzac once wrote of its effects, "everything is agitated . . . memories charge in". Earlier in the evening I went looking for the little sketchbook Anthea had left me from the box at the top of my closet that is filled with those kinds of mementoes, old letters and old photographs from my old past lives.

As I page through Anthea's sketchbook, there are the drawings just as I remembered them: my face, my mother, the trees. But there are three pages at the back I do not remember, and that I know were not there when Anthea pressed this into my hands some thirty years ago.

They could not have been, because only one is a self-portrait of Anthea as the child that I knew; in the other, she is a teenager, and in the final one, the adult Anthea of the paintings that have haunted me these long twelve months gone by. Anthea the child is happy and whole, but Anthea the teenager has fragmented, her face a Picasso-like reworking with features placed all wrong, and Anthea the adult is missing limbs—which ones, I cannot say for certain, because I cannot bear to look past the single moment in which my gaze falls upon it as I turn the page.

But I am even more distressed by the existence of the drawings themselves than by their content. I have turned on all the lights because I am concerned about what may be lurking round the edges of things. Head down, ignoring my peripheral vision. The silence around me is too much. Earplugs to deafen the silence are insufficient; I have turned up music as loud as I can bear and still the silence is all around the edges of everything.

It is not enough.

I think I should get into my car, I should drive away, maybe drive to Justine's, but some time ago, in an effort to ease the agitation, I began adding shots of whiskey to the coffee and now my mind and my body are simultaneously frantic but dull; my thoughts are racing, but they are taking twice as long to turn up at the place they are meant to be.

If I say her name, will she appear before me? Is she waiting even now in the next room, dressed in her baptismal robe, blaspheming in a blaze of heavenly sunlight that makes her look like an angel? And what of these demons she has birthed? A monstrous mother indeed; for they are all her progeniture, real or imagined.

I have decided I do not wish for her return. And so I sit here at my kitchen table, my back to the wall, eyes on the doorway, waiting as though I am under siege. Perhaps I am. I have turned on my webcam and have my laptop facing the door, and every few moments I pick up my phone and snap photos randomly about the room, about the walls and the ceiling. Anthea hated photographs. She will not come if she believes she may be captured in this way. At least, this is what I tell myself.

But I have just scrolled back through the last few photos taken and surely it is my thumb, a smudge on the lens, a trick of the light. Not someone on the edge of things. Not a woman ducking just out of range of the camera's focus.

*I'll see you later*, she said once, a lifetime ago.

It's the darkest part of the night, and later is right now.

# The Other Side

A few months after Adam disappeared, my phone started ringing and blinking his name at me. I snatched at it and knocked it off the table instead. When I finally fumbled it back into my hands and accepted the call it was with a string of swears before I gasped, "Adam! Where the hell are you?"

There was a moment of silence, and then a woman's voice said awkwardly, "Sorry, Mark, this is Lauren. Adam's sister."

I was speechless with rage and sorrow, and she had to have known I would be. "I'm sorry," she said again when I didn't reply, "I didn't think. I just saw your name in his phone and I . . . "

I had only met her a couple of times, a washed-out woman with a face that was somehow pudgy and hard at the same time. Adam had never got on with her, and I got the sense she didn't like me either. I'm pretty sure she'd thought we were lovers but it was never like that with me, or with Adam and me. Anyway, Adam had only fucked people he would never see again. Not that I was ever going to tell her that.

"I didn't know Adam didn't have his phone with him," I said, irrelevantly.

"I'm sorry," Lauren said yet again, and that was probably more than the total number of times she'd ever apologised for anything in her life up to that point. "I didn't know who else to call."

"About what?"

"It's Adam. I've seen him."

"What? Where? Did you go to him?" I was already shrugging into a jacket, but she said, "No, no, it isn't like that. Exactly."

"What exactly is it like?" I said, biting off the ends of the words, and she was silent for a beat. "Can you just meet me?" she said. "I can't really talk about it over the phone."

In fact, Lauren and Adam were twins, which made the fact I'd never met two siblings less alike even stranger. But that she chose to meet me in one of the most depressing cafés I've ever had the displeasure of visiting made me rethink their difference. That was all Adam: eating in terrible cafés, living in grim bedsits, drinking in pubs that hung the St. George's Cross and smelt of urine. He took a pleasure in it, you see—it was maybe his only source of pleasure. "Let's go on a picnic," he'd say, and two hours later you'd find yourself sitting with a spread in the middle of some godawful housing estate surrounded by feral children and their chavvy barely-not-children-themselves parents. By "you", of course, I mean me. I was generally terrified in those situations. Adam was exuberant. He had this idea that you could find the most profound beauty, even the sacred, in the ugliest places. You had to train yourself to look for it, he'd say.

It was what we feared, of course, those of us who knew him best. That he'd finally looked in the wrong place, or with the wrong person.

Lauren and I exchanged pleasantries, as though either of us cared how the other was doing. The waitress brought us cups of tea that tasted like they'd been made with dishwater. She seemed as reluctant to broach our purpose in being there as I was anxious to hear what she had to say. We sat for several minutes in silence until she finally said, "I saw him from the motorway."

"What?"

"It was just outside of the city," she said. "Out near that stretch of abandoned factories."

I said, "What?" again, more emphatically this time. And then: "Did you stop? How was he? Did you talk to him? How did he look?"

"He looked—" She couldn't speak for several seconds, then she lifted her face up to me and I was surprised to see her eyes shimmering with tears. "Beatific."

I wouldn't have thought Lauren would come up with a word like that. That she did, told me everything I needed to know. I was angry at her for wasting my time, but I told myself it wasn't her fault.

"I mean," she said, reading my silence, "it wasn't some kind of hallucination. It was him, solid as you are right now. He was there, he was really real. I couldn't stop, of course, but I got off and went back down the motorway and I couldn't see him. I got out and looked for him. I walked up through the brush and he wasn't there any more. I didn't know what to do. So I wrote a note for him. I weighted it with a rock and left it there and I went and told the police what I'd seen and now I'm telling you."

There was a pleading quality to her voice that angered me. She expected something from me, reassurance maybe, but I wasn't going to give it to her. I drank my tea in silence for a few minutes. Finally I said, "What do you want me to do?"

"I don't know," Lauren said. "You two were—I mean, you were closest to him. I thought it might mean something to you. Or you'd know what to do. Mark, he's alive."

She said it with such conviction I almost believed her. How I longed to believe her. To think Adam might come walking through the door at that very moment with that disarming grin of his, what a joke he'd played on us—but that would never happen, because Adam wasn't the joke-playing type. If Adam was gone, then Adam was dead—that was the four-letter word we wouldn't say to one another, and it felt like a betrayal to say it even to myself, but it was true.

"Will you just go and see?" Lauren said. "Will you?"

I don't know why I said I would. To get away from that awful cup of tea and out of that awful café and far from that awful sister of his. To get her to stop looking at me with those pleading eyes.

Because it was just the sort of place that Adam *would* be, only she couldn't possibly know that about him.

They were born, Adam said to me once, trying to kill each other. Her cord around his neck nearly strangled him.

As soon as they were free of the womb they'd been forced to share, they set out doing their best to ignore one another, and had done for thirty years. I knew Adam for a dozen years, and for the first few, I didn't even know he had a sister. There was just the two of them, too, no other family—their parents were dead, in circumstances Adam would never discuss with me, and they'd grown up in care. Adam never talked about his family, his childhood, or his personal life at all really.

We'd met at a gig. I don't really remember much about the night because I was drunk. I was also having a fight with my then-girlfriend, who stormed out at some point. Adam and I were drinking and talking and laughing and then, much later, we were sitting on a disused railway bridge with our feet dangling, smoking fags, and Adam started telling me about something he called the edgelands. He said it was something people had known about for a long time, since the Industrial Revolution first created such places. It was a woman named Marion Shoard who had dreamt up the word "edgelands", but he said he believed it had been given to her.

"What do you mean, 'given to her'?" I asked.

Adam said, "The edgelands are liminal places where you can tap into other things."

I didn't know what liminal meant, either. I was starting to feel seriously out of my depth.

I said, "What's that?"

Adam said quietly, "Thresholds. Not here or there. We're in one now."

I'd been slumped against the struts of the bridge, but when Adam said that I sat up, suddenly feeling clear-headed and scared. Adam went on. "Anything can happen in the edgelands. They're blighted places, and that makes them magical. Ruined places. Ruined people. That's what interests me."

We stayed sitting there for a long time and shared a joint between us. Nothing like the strange stuff Adam was talking about happened to us though. I got back home around dawn—I still lived with my parents in those days—and later on my girlfriend rang me and demanded to know whether I was queer, going off with that bloke like I did. I said as I remembered it she was the one who'd left. She said I was dodging the question. Then she broke up with me.

Funny that I don't even remember her name now.

After that I started running into Adam all the time. We'd see each other at gigs and then later we started making more deliberate plans together. It wasn't until a couple of years later though, after we got a flat together, that he talked about the edgelands again.

Adam used to tell me about his dreams. I know that makes him sound like a tedious fucker, but somehow the way Adam described them, they were always gripping. I used to wonder if maybe he was lying, because nobody could remember their dreams in such detail or have dreams that were so compelling, so meaningful. That was another thing about Adam: he was one of the most honest people I've ever known. Sure, he didn't open up much, but if he told you something, it was bound to be the truth. I don't think he was capable of saying something that wasn't.

One morning, a couple of months after we'd first got the flat, I was sitting bleary-eyed on the couch with a bowl of Weetabix. He came into the room and sat down right next to me. He started talking and I felt vaguely annoyed because I was hungover and had the feeling this was going to be a long one. Unlike Adam, I wasn't unemployed. I had to get to my job at Wax Me Records.

"Do you remember when we first met? When I took you out to that railway bridge, and I told you about the edgelands?"

I said no, because I was hoping that would discourage him. Of course, being Adam, he didn't miss a beat.

"They're the places that aren't city but aren't countryside either," he said. "Where you find disused railways and abandoned factories and burnt-out cars. Some of them are poison. Toxic. Wastelands. Only they aren't waste—well, they are, but that's the point. They aren't anything, they're lost places. Last night I dreamed I was in the edgelands.

"I was walking through tall grass and muck. I knew the muck was poisonous and I could feel it sucking at my shoes as I went, it was so real, but it was like something was telling me to keep going. I was moving toward these rusted metal girders in the distance. It seemed important that I reach them even though I didn't know why."

I said, "I'm late for work." I started putting on my Vans.

"Wait," Adam said, and put a hand on my arm. That stopped me. Adam never touched me. He wasn't a touching-you kind of guy. "Listen," he said. "You can go in a minute. I need to tell someone about this." I was shocked to see he had tears in his eyes. "I kept moving but it was getting harder to walk, I kept slipping. When I looked down, what I saw underfoot were—things like little children's hands, floating in the muck and all twisted up with bits of barbed wire. I started pulling them out, like I thought the children might still be attached and I could save them, but it was just their hands. At first I couldn't work out where I'd gone wrong. I had gone to that place looking for something beautiful. And then as I went on, the severed hands started seeming beautiful to me. At the same time, I knew that was wrong, that something had gone wrong in me to think that. And then I finally reached the girders and they weren't metal at all, they were made of flesh.

"It was like all the suffering that made the edgelands, all those buildings and factories sucking the life out of the land only to be forgotten as well, had vomited up these things. The harder I looked for something beautiful the more horrific it all became until I couldn't tell the difference any longer." His voice cracked. "I'm scared, Mark. I feel like I took a wrong turn somewhere. I'm afraid of what I'm capable of."

I said, "I don't understand what you're trying to tell me."

"Neither do I." He retreated then. His hand dropped, and he got up from the sofa. "I'm sorry. Go to work."

"Look, if you need me—"

"I don't need anybody," he said, and he walked out of the front door of the flat and slammed it behind him. I went after him, right away, but he was nowhere to be seen. It was like he could vanish at will, even in those days.

❦

When I got back to my flat after meeting Lauren, my girlfriend Polly was waiting there for me. She hadn't properly moved in but she had a key and was there at least as often as she was at her own place.

She was sitting on the sofa watching something that she used the remote to stop as soon as I came in the room. She said, "We need to talk."

I said, "Oh for fuck's sake." That wasn't the best response, was it? But it wasn't just because those four words strung together manage to be ominous, tedious and clichéd all at once. It was the snap back into my everyday life and the realisation of how little present I was in it and how little I cared about it. I wondered how long that had been going on, but in an idle way.

I said, "I can't talk right now," and Polly said, "Why not?" I didn't say anything, and she said, "That's the whole point, Mark. This *is* the talk. That you don't tell me anything, you don't let me in. You keep me on a need-to-know basis. It's like I'm not really a part of your life."

Polly was a beautiful girl. She had honey-coloured hair and skin that just glowed and she liked sex and she was agreeable and easy to be around and she was the kind of girl your friends like too, so that when you broke up with her, mates would all think you were mad and you wouldn't know how to explain it because how do you explain absence? You break up with people—at least people you've been with for a while, like Polly and me—*because* of something, something one of you does or says, or because you have some profound disagreement over whether or not to get married or have kids or buy a flat. Or those are the reasons you give anyway. Because you can't say to people *it was because something wasn't there*. What, they would ask. Love? Commitment? Sex? Affection? No, none of those things. Passion? That wasn't right either, that described something fleeting and what I was reaching for was the opposite of fleeting.

"What is it?" Polly said. "Is it because you were single for so long? Do you just not know how to let someone into your life?" She reached out for me, to touch me, but her hand fell away into nothing.

☙

There was something I hadn't told Lauren. I hadn't told anyone, not the police, not any of my and Adam's mutual friends. I told myself it didn't matter because it wasn't relevant.

I got a letter from Adam a day or two after he was last seen. No, it isn't right to call it a letter. The envelope was addressed to me in his handwriting. Adam had never sent me anything in his life, and as soon as I received it, I rang him up to talk to him about it, to ask him why he'd sent it to me and what it meant, but of course there was no answer. At the time I didn't think anything of it. It was only when a day and another day passed and I couldn't reach him that I began to realise that something was wrong, and by then, other people had too.

The other strange thing was that when I received it, I hadn't seen or spoken to him for a while. We weren't on the outs, but Adam and I would go through periods where we'd just be out of touch for a while, busy with our own lives, and then we'd come back into contact. But he'd never made contact like this before.

When I opened the envelope, a single slip of paper fell out and drifted to the floor. I picked it up, and this is what I read:

"This dream came in the spring, when I was nineteen—a time when I felt emotionally confused and lonely. I was standing among a group of people in a railway station, on an outdoor platform. It was early evening; the air was cool. The people with me weren't strangers, but I didn't know them well. They might have included friends and colleagues. They were bickering and pacing, like any group of travellers waiting for a late train. The atmosphere was sullen. I felt out of place, though it was a situation I was used to.

"By chance, I glanced across the platform. Through the bars of a luggage rack, I saw a young man of my own age. He was sitting alone on a large suitcase with his hands spread beside him, gazing at the tracks. His face was pale; his hair was somewhere between brown and blond. There was a quiet stillness about him. He didn't look like anyone I knew in real life. I thought I knew why he was alone.

"The evening light seemed brighter there or at least less cluttered. I picked up my suitcase and crossed the platform to sit beside him. He looked at me. Our hands touched, held. No one from the group I'd left came after me. The world behind us ceased to exist. We waited, together, for the train that was going in the opposite direction to my planned journey. It grew darker on the platform, but the lamplight watched over us.

"Still more embarrassing than recalling this dream is recalling that I woke in tears, gripped by a virtual infatuation that hurt for days. It wasn't an erotic dream; it was a dream about being in love, which is much scarier and harder to make compromises with. And it wasn't just a dream about 'sexuality' either: the image of crossing over, of changing direction, had other meanings which I'm still learning about. Really important dreams don't come true; you go on dreaming them, and they change you."

And at the very bottom of the page, three words: "in the edgelands".

I went to the place where Lauren said she'd seen him. I got a city bus part of the way and then got out and walked. It was a blighted area, all right, just the type of place Adam *would* vanish into. Brush instead of any real vegetation, and hulking monstrous buildings that might have been abandoned twenty-five or a hundred years ago for all I knew. It was like the motorway buzzing through it had rendered it all but invisible. It wasn't a real place at all any longer but a place to pass through. I didn't know what any of it had been once upon a time—why would I? Why would anyone? It was the kind of place you forgot even while you were looking at it. Adam would have known.

I spooked myself, just a little, thinking of the little severed hands of Adam's dream, not literally expecting them of course but it did occur to me that this was the kind of place where people dumped bodies, and I wondered what it would be like to find one, some murdered man or woman, battered or shot or knifed, exposed to the elements for who knew how long, their empty corpse waiting for acknowledgement. I felt that being discovered by me would somehow be a disappointment.

I walked for a long time. It grew cold, and a biting wind went on the attack, so I huddled deeper inside my coat and scarf. I didn't expect to see Adam and yet somehow I couldn't bring myself to leave, worried that to do so prematurely would be to abandon him altogether. I also wanted to tell Lauren with sincerity that I had tried.

As the day wore on, I was unsurprised to come across a set of train tracks. I followed them for some time before the dying day and a fierce wind finally drove me back onto the road and in search of another bus. I think if I'd followed those tracks long enough I might have found the abandoned station they passed through, and dull as the day was, it might have been warmer and lighter there, but I don't know, and I don't know what I would have done, or seen, or been after that.

Still later, back at my flat, I slipped into bed next to Polly. We were still together, in that state a relationship reaches where you know its days are numbered but neither of you has the courage yet to end it. What Adam would have called *liminal*. She was sound asleep. I reached out to touch her. She liked being woken up for sex; we had fucked, wordlessly, countless times in the dark, in the middle of the night, like that. I think it made her feel like she could shed inhibitions but I don't know because we never talked about it. She didn't wake when I touched her that night, though. She didn't even stir, so deep was she in dreams. I wondered what she dreamed about. We never talked about that either.

The letter from Adam had been startling to me in more ways than one. Of course, there was the strangeness of receiving it in the first place, but even more, I was surprised by the longing that suffused it. I'd never met any of Adam's boyfriends because he never had any—though he had as much sex as anyone I've ever known, it was purely anonymous, entirely recreational. The idea of Adam ever falling in love with anyone, let alone that he appeared to have been so secretly consumed by a desire to do so, startled me. In a way it made me feel like I'd never really known him at all, but I don't know that people ever do. Know one another, I mean.

After I finally fell asleep, I dreamed as well, and I remembered the dream the following day, which was unusual for me. I was back in the edgelands. I was walking with someone who I thought was Polly, though I wasn't sure, and Adam was on the other side of me. It looked different than it had when I'd been there. The only way I can think to describe it is if you've ever woken early someplace that is not a city, where it is bright and the dew is glistening on twigs and grass and leaves and makes everything look like glass. It should have been beautiful, but all I felt was fear. I felt big and clumsy and like I might break something, and I felt like that would be the worst thing in the world. I didn't know what would happen, but it would be terrible. I wanted to tell Adam and the person who I thought was Polly what I was afraid of, but every time I tried to talk to them it was as if they couldn't hear me. The same glass seemed to separate us, and although I was between them, they could hear each other but I couldn't hear either of them. They were talking and laughing with one another and neither of them seemed afraid of anything breaking. I began to think maybe it wasn't Polly next to me at all, and I wanted to look at who it was instead, but I was afraid of that too. I finally mounted the courage to do so and when I did, I saw that it was me. I was so frightened I didn't know what to do. I didn't understand what it meant: had I split in two, or was I not who I believed myself to be, or both of those things?

When I finally woke, morning sun streaming through my window, I didn't know where I was for long moments. Next to me, Polly was still breathing softly, still dreaming. I was as well; I believed that I was made of glass, and that if I moved, I would shatter. Yet at the same time it seemed critical that I reach across the gulf between us and touch her. Like the boy in Adam's dream, she was awash in a golden light, and yet unlike in his dream, I could not move. I could not reach her; I could not cross to the other side.

*For Joel Lane*

## The Secret Woods

Nothing had changed. The old roads and the old houses and the old woods were just as she remembered them. Uncannily so, for what was more unreliable than memory, and yet here were her memories untouched and real as anything—as her hands before her on the steering wheel, as the bland pop music piped from the speakers of the rental car. Down then she went, down into the valley, down into her past. What a terrible thing, to learn that one's memories were real and true, for that meant they could be believed, and what had saved her throughout her adult life had been the certainty that everything she could recall was false.

Pan—oh yes, she knew Pan, of course she did. She had always known him; he had always belonged to her, and she to him. In her childhood, he had been a child as well, feral and irresistible as are all forbidden things, innocently amoral, full of tricks, fascinated with bodily effluvium—blood, piss, shit—capricious and often cruel. Even when he sent her home in tears she'd forgive him by the following day, racing out into the woods to play with him again—and what play it was! Imagine if you would a god as your favourite playmate, and the things he could show you. Imagine breaking open an ancient and still living tree, imagine breaking into the very heart of it. Imagine what you would inhale at that heart: aeons coiled deep inside, summers lost five hundred years or more, traces of the fertile soil that nursed the seed when the land was younger (but still so very old). Her mother scolded her for going off on her own, for avoiding the company of her sister and of other children, but what normal child could compete?

Then everything had changed in the space of a season, after a winter that had seemed filled with bad dreams and arguments, but at the end of it she was older, and she did not need imaginary playmates and made-up secrets. She sensed a different kind of power now, a power that rose like musk off the palms of her hands. She'd turned thirteen, after all. She liked a boy at school. She didn't need to run like something savage through the woods and braid pieces of kudzu through her hair and pretend to be queen of something wild and invisible and secret. She had been a little girl before and now she was a woman. Her legs grew long and her feet mashed up inside too-small shoes and her chest that had been flat in the fall grew breasts sometime in the months between. Where had all that flesh and bone and skin come from, to make all the parts of her body longer and bigger so quickly? It seemed monstrous, making new flesh where before there had been none at all.

Spring was coming. She was older now; her body proved it. Spring would be different this time.

Home. *Home*. Home.

The word had held no allure for her for so very long, and suddenly she was here and suddenly she wanted never again to leave. It was all in a rush, just like that, like twenty years of unfelt emotions surging to the surface.

Twenty years. She would know exactly how long even if she was not being asked over and over: *How long is it since we've seen you, Diana?* Really? *How can it be that long?* How could it not be? How could it not be a lifetime? How could she be back here? How could any of it be?

Her childhood home, the house itself, was one thing that bore little resemblance to her recollections of it, but that made sense: her sister and her sister's husband had thoroughly remodeled the place. Inside, the layout had changed so much that it might be any house, not the one from her memory, and they had done the outside as well: trimmed back the forest and landscaped the front and back yards. She sensed the lingering ghosts of felled trees behind her as she stood at the edge of the yard and gazed into the forest.

She felt grimly glad about the trees that had been cut down.

Behind her, in the house but audible from out here, her sister's anniversary party was in full swing. Ten years together; Kristen said it hardly seemed long enough to throw a party about but they'd had a courthouse wedding, neither of them having any family to attend, and wanted a real celebration. And with Diana coming home, that was reason enough also.

A door slammed, and behind her, her nephew cried, "Aunt Diana! Aunt Diana, Mama says you need to come on in! Daddy's talking now!"

To her sister's three children, two nieces and a nephew, who had only seen her on Skype at the Christmases when she bothered at all, she might have been a celebrity, an alien, an almost-unreal being dropped in from unknown parts. Unlike the adults, they stared at her openly: at the tattoos, at the piercings in her face, and the way she was dressed and at her hair and all the ways she didn't belong. To everyone else, she was the prodigal. Behind their smiles and their greetings she wondered what they must think of her. Perhaps they did not think of her at all. Perhaps they thought her dreadful. If only they knew. If only.

Inside, a dining room table was laden with appetizers from Costco, little quiches and chicken tenders and egg rolls and vegetable trays with dips. Her sister's husband Marc was raising his glass and saying some words about his beloved wife, words she forgot as soon as she heard them, but then what did she know? She didn't love anyone. Everyone was drinking a little too much champagne and laughing a little too loudly, but no, really, those were just the judgments of a snotty teenage Diana, the last role she'd played as part of a family unit (well—not the very last—but that was not to be thought of). She had to learn how to be adult Diana in the space of a single afternoon among people she had only ever been a child around.

Everyone was having a perfectly nice time. This was nice, and her sister was nice, and her sister's family was nice, and the house, what they'd done with it, was nice, and she, too, was going to be nice, and then she was going to excuse herself from this nice but ill-advised trip back down memory lane and take herself back home, back to her *real* home, not here, to the din and the smells and the energy of the city where everything was man-made and nothing was real. She could not actually say when she had last been in the countryside. Never. She never went.

Then, in the forest, she had been Diana the huntress. As a child, she had read about the goddess she liked to think of as her namesake, and when she was with Pan, she had almost believed it—when you were friends with a god, why not be a god yourself?—and afterwards she was only ordinary Diana, just a girl, just a woman, the moon and the forest and the whole of creation lost to her. And why should it not be?

After all, it had all been make-believe. It must have been. She was grateful for a childhood of benign neglect, that she had managed to not be attended by an army of concerned parents and psychologists and teachers, that she was allowed an imaginary friend rather than being shunted off to a therapist and medicated into compliance. Oh, just imagine how angry *that* would have made Pan. What he might have done.

Because what he did was bad enough.

She had told herself she was not going to smoke while she was there, but that was before she had actually arrived, before she was able to take the true measure of what she was up against. As she stepped outside again, this time into the front yard where she would not face the forest but the road and thus felt a bit safer, she confessed it to her sister shamefacedly—wasn't smoking something normal, decent people no longer did? It was only when Marc joined that it occurred to her that very possibly, she had not the faintest ideas about how normal, decent people behaved, or anything at all really.

"It must feel weird for you being back here," Marc said, after first getting a light off her.

She shrugged, then remembered that teenage Diana was not allowed to make any more appearances and found her voice. "Yeah, it really is." It was a little bit easier to talk to Marc because he was someone entirely new, someone she had not known from before. "I didn't think it would be this weird, really. Or maybe I did. I kind of don't know what I thought."

"I really appreciate you coming here," Marc said. "Kristen appreciates it. She was so happy you said you would. I know it's not your kind of thing."

She lowered her cigarette and quietly appraised him. She and her sister could not have been more different. Kristen had never left home, never would. Her whole world was the town where they'd grown up, her family, and her job as a respiratory technician at the hospital in town. Marc was from—somewhere, Diana couldn't even remember where now, out west maybe?—and had done two tours of duty in Iraq and had a calm ex-soldier's acceptance about him. Maybe you'd seen some things, done some things. So had he. Want to forgive each other for them and go have a beer?

She said, "God, I could use a beer."

He laughed. "You should've said something. You didn't strike me as the champagne type. Hold this." He handed her his cigarette, went back inside, and came out with a six-pack of Miller Lite dangling from one hand. "Here." He pulled one off and handed it to her and opened one for himself, setting the other four at their feet. "If you can call this beer. Kristen likes it." They touched the two cans together in a show of solidarity and drank silently.

Then she said, "My parents—" at the same time that he said, "Your parents—"

They both stopped, and then he resumed. "I wish I'd met them. The way Kristen talks about them."

"Well, at the time, they were just, you know. Mom and Dad. We were kids. It's looking back that I can see how special they were—how much they loved each other. It used to embarrass us, the way he indulged her and how demonstrative they were and all. I always told myself they'd have wanted to go together like that. Well, not like that, but you know. It helped to think that, kind of."

You had to tell yourself those things. You couldn't think about it any further, think about whether they knew, whether one was alive longer than the other, did they suffer, was there terror, was there grief. You had to tell yourself it was over in an instant, existence winked out just like that. You couldn't bear anything else.

"I know," he said, and of course he would know. She could see it in his eyes that were older and sadder than the face in which they were set.

"So," she said, "I left. Took off. Couldn't deal with it. I guess it was an awful thing to do. Kristen was my little sister. She was only thirteen and I was seventeen. Older sisters are supposed to take care of younger ones."

"It wasn't your fault," Marc said. "None of it was your fault."

She said, "No, all of it was."

The boy she had picked—that was the worst of it. Not that there was anything wrong with him. But if it had been true love, or at least something she thought was true love, she might have been able to excuse herself in the days and the months and the years that followed. It was nothing like true love. It wasn't even true lust really. He was a boy she'd made out with a few times, nothing more, and she was curious and felt like the last virgin left on the face of the earth. It hadn't even been that great—it hadn't been horrible and painful like some people said it would be, there hadn't been blood and agony, but it also hadn't been especially rapturous. It had been nice. That was all. Nice.

No, even that wasn't the worst of it. The worst was that she had known what she was doing. She knew it would anger Pan. She knew, and she didn't care, and she didn't think about the consequences because she was seventeen and because she was stupid and because she was selfish and then her parents were dead and now they were still dead and it was all her fault.

Had she known what would be, the first time Pan showed her the dryads, those mad impetuous tree-spirits, she would not have laughed with delight; she would not have tried to embrace them, tried to *be* them. She would have tried to kill them. She would have razed the land, cut down every tree by hand if necessary and driven them out or died doing so.

They had been savage, yes, but everything about Pan and Pan's world had been savage, and she had loved that. She had not imagined that Pan, in his jealousy, would unleash the dryads, that they would do his bidding and sacrifice themselves, and that storms would rage and trees would fall, in the end crushing the roof of her parents' car and their fragile human bodies trapped within.

Marc seemed like the kind of guy you could talk to, the kind of guy who would listen without judgement, but there was no way she could tell him *that* story. So instead she reached for another beer.

"Kristen never held it against you," he said. "She never saw it the way you say. She didn't think you had a responsibility like that or anything. She missed you, but she didn't blame you."

"She should have then." She needed to be careful. Alcohol would loosen her tongue. She avoided it most of the time; and not just alcohol but almost any class of drugs. She had to stay clear-headed at all times both to keep herself safe and to keep herself from talking. She'd made that mistake a few times, early on, and learned her lesson quickly. Even people on the fringes like gutterpunks and squatters or people who imagined themselves there like burners and wannabe artists would start shunning you when you went on and on too long about your friend the goat-footed god, about murderous dryads and magical dances and childhood secrets sown in deceit that felt like innocence, or maybe they were the same thing. It was easier to believe she was unhinged than in any of it being true, and if she kept the madness to herself everything would be okay.

"I don't know why I came here," she said. "It's so dangerous for me to be here. I guess the guilt got the best of me this time." Maybe it was already too late. The words rolled off her tongue before she could stop them.

"I know something about guilt," Marc said mildly. "Sometimes it's right on the money, but you know, sometimes it lies to you. Especially when you're seventeen years old and you think the world revolves around you and so everything must be your fault. Even tornadoes."

"You don't understand," she said. "There's stuff you don't know about. It *was* my fault."

He went on like she wasn't even talking, and now she was hearing him through a red haze of rage. How dare he presume to know. "So maybe you had a fight with your parents beforehand or something and it all gets mixed up in your head with the trauma and all and you come out the other side convinced that something you did made it happen. You even try to make it logical maybe, tell yourself if they hadn't been upset at you, they'd have been paying attention, things would have been different. Maybe it's easier to think it's your fault than to think that anybody you love can be taken from you at any moment like it's the whim of God."

"Are you two ever planning on joining us again?"

That was Kristen, at the front door, leaning round it and smiling at them, her face open and guileless—happy her long lost sister and her husband, two of the people she loved most in the world, seemed to be getting along. Diana looked at her and the rage evaporated; fear stormed in to replace it. She was so unbearably vulnerable—they all were—and so unsafe. And she knew suddenly, as though Kristen had told her, even though she hadn't said a thing: she's pregnant again.

When she was little, Kristen had always said she wanted a big family, loads of kids. Three kids now, another on the way, maybe more after that.

It was no safe place for them, here at the threshold, in a place where worlds faded into one another in a way worlds never should. She had given these creatures names that made sense to her from a book she'd had as a child, *Gods and Goddesses of the Ancient World*, but only because naming them made them seem safe. She had no idea what they were, what they wanted, *why* they were. Or why her. And if she had known, surely it would have made no sense at all anyway.

The seduction of their enchantments. The terror of their rage.

Kristen and Marc were both talking to her now, but their words were coming through to her as though the air were a bad transmitter, buzzing and sparking and expiring before they reached her. What they were saying to her didn't matter. They had to stay safe. She had to keep them safe, whatever it took. She had failed people who loved her once and she would not again. She said, "I need some fresh air. I need to go for a walk," and she thought one of them said her name but she could not be sure and she was in back of the house, across the yard, and she stepped across the threshold. She stepped into the forest.

The moment she did, everything changed.

She still had every notebook in which she'd written down all the important things she'd learned. Throughout childhood she'd filled them with writing and sketches; now they seemed embarrassing and painful, but to destroy them or throw them out was unthinkable. A day had come when she'd written some last words in them and put them away under her bed, putting away childish things. She had only made the mistake of looking back at them once, as a teenager, and she'd sworn then to never do so again. That one time she'd read them, aghast at the things she'd written there and the things she had forgotten and the things she had lost, and she'd raised a tear-stained face hours later and vowed to seek it all back out again, but then the phone had rung, her friend Amy calling, and the spell had been broken. She had been tugged back from the brink.

That had frightened her. It was one thing to think she'd been an imaginative, dreamy child; it was another entirely to think she might have been a mad one, that she'd set down that madness methodically in evocative words and pictures, and that that madness could claim her once more if she were again to let it too close.

All children were mad, she told herself. Wasn't childhood itself a state of insanity? The things you did, and the things you believed! Growing up was simply a matter of coming to some sort of consensus with everyone else about what those beliefs would be.

By her seventeenth summer, Pan had retreated to the ragged edges of childhood memory. She dreamed of him but then she dreamed of many things. She rarely went into the woods any longer because she was busy, because there was school and friends and movies and boys and all the sweet unexplored possibilities of sex. When she did venture near the forest she sometimes caught the rank and rutting scent of him, but that was impossible, she had made him up, nothing else could be true.

And yet the notebooks had been among the few items she took with her when she fled, and she had kept them close to her all these years, unread; she carried a few with her wherever she went. It was a way of keeping something close that seemed vital but unspeakable. Now, in the forest, she scrabbled through her bag for them, pulled one out, and let it fall open to a random page.

*We found a blackberry bush and fed one another, but the berries were overripe, squashed and rotting, bursting and pecked to pieces by birds. My mouth was still purple when I woke up the next morning. I said it was all real, but it might have been a dream.*

It might have. In those days, real and dream had been relative states to her; working out which was one and which the other had seemed a matter of little import. What did it matter when the dreams were more real than the world itself?

She turned the page.

*I liked going to Mr. Lee's house up the road to see his goats. I went there today and his wife told me they were all dead! But I just saw them the other day! I started crying, I couldn't help it. I loved those little goats. She said it was because they had some kind of disease. Then she said he slit their throats, one by one. Why would she tell me that? About that time Mr. Lee came in. He's this real old farmer, he saw me crying and normally he's real nice to me but this time he wasn't, he said I should go. He said he did the right thing but it wasn't something I could or should understand. I was crying so hard I could barely talk like when you're a little kid you cry until you make yourself sick and also because I was scared for him and his wife too, like what might happen to them for him doing that, and I was crying and stumbling back toward home and so I went into the woods and Pan was there and I told him what happened, I had to, and he said he knew and that it was because people were afraid of him still without knowing why or even that he existed and sometimes they went crazy and did crazy things and all the time he was telling me that, he looked more like a goat than a person. Then he changed again and said I should forget it and I asked him not to hurt the Lees and he said why would he do that, and we went down by the creek and the dryads and the naiads taught me another game that I can't write down here or speak about but they let me draw them so I did.*

She couldn't remember what had happened to the Lees, or even if they were still around. She would ask Kristen when she got back to the house.

Her drawings had not been at all representational; there was a sense of movement about the lines but no figures depicted.

Another page:

*Today I tried to show Kristen some of the games. I showed her the one about the stone and the sky and the moss and Mom even came in and watched for a little bit and laughed at the dancing part and asked what we were doing. Then Kristen started crying like the big baby she is and said she didn't like it anymore and Mom made me stop playing it with her even though we were just getting to the good part.*

What was the game about the stone and the sky and the moss? Diana couldn't remember. She couldn't remember trying to bring Kristen into any of it either. There was still so much she couldn't remember.

She was deep in the woods now. The forest had come alive around her, and she could hear the trees waking up and stretching their branches toward the sky. Did they remember her? She could wait until they did.

But as she waited, doubt seeded and grew within her.

Everything had changed from that spring, just as she had known it would. Her body had changed and she had changed, and so Pan had changed and so the whole world as she had known it up to then had changed as well. The very thought of venturing into the forest had begun to seize her with an inchoate fear. She bled along with the cycles of the moon, she could track her own waxing and waning with a lunar calendar and then she later read that was a myth, that the moon had nothing at all to do with the rhythms of a woman's body. But then Pan was a myth as well, wasn't he, and yet so much realer than anything, realer than the school bus and the clock ticking down the minutes in math class and the buzzing fluorescent classroom lights. Real as he was, he receded as all memories do. And as they abandoned one another, she nearly forgot him until that terrible night.

This was her own myth, the one she had always told herself, but had she not just been an exceptionally imaginative child? She felt foolish now, standing in the woods with the pages of her notebooks fluttering in the breeze, having run away from her sister's party and in doing so made the scene anyway that she'd so hoped to avoid. The only myths in her life were her own, the complicated lies she invented to explain why she was the way she was. A lifetime of celibacy, of not making things, of loving no one, of piercing and painting her own body when the urge to create something became too desperate because anything else might invite the panic, the pandemonium, and the loss that would surely follow. And telling herself at the same time that she believed none of it. Holding two conflicting beliefs at the same time was the easiest thing in the world; everyone did it; why did anyone say otherwise? But the madness had not been something from outside her that she'd had to avoid at all costs lest she conjure it up again. It had been embedded deep inside, delusions of gods and grandeur hiding the terror of a loss of control.

She let the notebook slip from her hands and lie where it landed in the dead leaves. All of it was false. Marc was right. She was not to blame, and never had been.

"You're not real," she said. "You never were."

The trees trembled and shook around her. A wind was coming up, a summer afternoon thunderstorm threatening. She should get back before she was drenched.

She should, she thought, be relieved, but she was not. *It wasn't your fault, none of it was your fault.* What did that matter when she had sacrificed her life to the belief that it was? And what did any of it say about her? There was something wrong with her. There had been since childhood.

*What she might have been. What she might have become.*

The notebook had fallen open where she dropped it, and as she bent down to pick it up, the words swam up at her, words she had not seen in twenty years, since she set them down and closed the book for the last time.

Here was another thing she could not remember: writing anything down in the aftermath of that terrible night. Had it not been so clearly her own familiar messy scribbles there on the page before her, spotted with ink blots from her beloved fountain pen, she would not have believed it.

The first fat drops of rain spattered down then and smeared the page, and suddenly the sky cracked open and the deluge was upon her. She snatched at the notebook but it was already too late; the pages were a sodden mess in seconds but in the end it did not matter because the past had come flooding back to her in all its vengeful fury.

On that night twenty years ago, she hadn't gone home. The boy—she couldn't even remember his name—had dropped her off at her house, but it had been dark. No one home, her parents out to dinner in town, Kristen sleeping over at a friend's, and she hadn't gone inside; she had gone walking instead. The moon had been full and the night had been warm and she'd wondered if she were still herself or if she'd been turned into something different.

Looking back, she had always remembered herself as fearful on that night, but that had not been the case, had it? She'd been many things, but fearful was not one of them.

She had been at once different and not-different in the same way Pan was real and not-real. The crescent moon had been high and bright and silver, and the night was hot and still though she could feel the storm on its way, gathering its forces, and she knew it would be a bad one which meant a good one; she adored thunderstorms.

Most of all what she remembered was that she had felt so *powerful*. In her mind she spoke to Pan: *I don't belong to you. I don't belong to anyone.* Heat lightning illuminated the sky though clouds rolled in with the coming storm and obscured her moon. The air crackled with electricity. The stillness was swept away; gusts of wind tossed the treetops and then fierce sheets of rain drenched her. It was a glorious storm.

She had conjured it all on her own, she had drawn it down from the heavens, and the thunder shook the earth and then the lightning struck a nearby tree and the impact knocked her off her feet. Only then did she realise it had gone wrong, it was too much, its fury was out of control. The shrieking wind ripped branches off trees and flung them down at her. She clung to a tree trunk and called out for them to help her, Pan and the dryads and all the others, but they would not come forth, and still the storm raged.

She thought she would be sucked into the very sky itself. The ground shook beneath her and the wind tore at her and if she lifted an outstretched hand before her eyes she could not see it through the lashing rain. The storm lasted forever. It was without beginning or end. Her terror turned to exhaustion, to resignation, almost to boredom: the monotony of destruction.

When its fury was finally spent to nothing but a steady drizzle of rain, she had risen and stumbled home. The house remained still and dark. Somewhere not a quarter of a mile away up on the road her parents were already dead—or so the emergency services said, though they probably told everyone their loved ones "died instantly"—and it seemed like the sort of thing she could have sensed, should have known, but she'd had no inkling. She'd been both exhausted and exhilarated, and she found her notebooks and opened one for the first time in years and wrote the lines of a poem she'd once memorised for school. *Pan is dead! Pan is dead! The great god Pan is dead!*

She had not really thought him dead, exactly—did gods die?—but she had sensed that there had been yet another change. She had towelled herself dry, changed clothes, got a Coke out of the fridge and sat on the front porch for a long time, watching the rain, and only then did she begin to notice the lateness of the hour, and that her parents were not yet home. The hand on her watch crawled past eleven-thirty and then midnight and she could no longer tell herself there was nothing to worry about; it wasn't just that her father had never in her entire memory gone to bed later than ten o'clock, but also that nothing was open this late in her small town even if he'd thrown caution to the winds. And yet she felt almost embarrassed as she dialled the emergency number, because nothing could be wrong. Things like that didn't just go wrong. She didn't know what to say when the dispatcher answered: "Um. I know this sounds weird, but, um, I don't know where my parents are?"

Was this the very tree she had clung to that night? Had the past walked her back through the years for a reprise? If so, the past was in error. She had not been timid in years, and she had nothing at all to lose.

Where she could not control the storm she could control herself. Each eruption of thunder and lightning caused the ground to quake. She could not see past the streaming rain.

The dead wet leaves slipped beneath her feet and the wind threatened to shove her to her knees and still she pressed on. Yet the storm's fury was not sustainable. In time its thunder quieted, its great gusts dissipated, and even the rain diminished. Back at the house, they would be worried about her, but they would be safe. This would not be a storm like that one had been.

They had to be safe, because she could not go to them.

These woods were more familiar to her than the streets round her apartment back in the city where she'd lived for years, as familiar as her own body. Pan's grove was deep in the heart of the forest. Everything there was so much richer and deeply felt. She could taste the warm, moist soil and the rain and the sunlight it absorbed and the decay it was cycling back into life and would later welcome once again in death, over and over, until the end of everything.

Softly, she said, "Pan is dead! The great god Pan is dead!"

But he was not, the great goat-footed beast, the savage child, the carnal youth, and nor was she, in spite of all her efforts to disappear. The world beyond them might be though, or not; she no longer cared.

She sank to the earth and for a long time, simply lay there. When she spoke at last, it was in the languages and the ways that they had taught her, the vocabulary she'd said she'd forgotten or said never was, a language which had lain dormant under her tongue, a language she'd always used when she dreamed.

Home. *Home.* Home.

Nothing had changed. The old words and the old rituals and the old ways were all waiting for her to find them again and call them back, just as she remembered them. What could be more reliable than memory, for she would no more have forgotten them than she would have forgotten her own name. They belonged to her now too, and she to them.

She would remember them forever, older than the earth, more ancient than the stars, the language that spoke all the beginnings into being.

Above the rain-drenched grove, the sun burst through the clouds and soaked her limbs in warmth, and in the woods beyond were shadows: darkness and penumbra.

# *Knots*

Sandra said, "How do things always get tangled up like this?"

She held up twisted ear buds in one hand and a snarled length of ethernet in the other.

Bastian shrugged. "They just do."

"But *how*?" It bugged her. She stared at them like they would supply her with an answer. "When I was a kid, I read books about these little people who lived in our houses. Borrowers. Maybe we have Borrowers?"

Bastian didn't crack a smile, or even acknowledge that she'd said anything more really. He just went on looking at his phone.

Sandra started untwisting the earbuds. It was maddening. How could they loop themselves into knots when they were just lying on a dresser overnight or sitting in a drawer?

"It's proof we really are living in a simulation," she said. "There's no logical explanation for how they do this to themselves when they're just on a table. It's impossible."

Silence.

"I'm leaving you. Also, I meant to tell you, the dog ran away a little while ago."

If he was only pretending not to listen, the second would get his attention even if the first didn't. He went on mindlessly stabbing at his phone.

Maybe talking about tangled cords wasn't her most *interesting* conversational gambit, Sandra acknowledged, but Jesus Christ. A little effort wouldn't go awry.

I will leave him, she thought. I will, I will. Soon. And when I do I won't tell him. I'll just go.

A thump as Barney jumped off the sofa onto the floor in the next room and then the clatter of his nails as he ran into the dining room where they sat at the table with the remains of breakfast between them. Bastian put down his phone, smiling broadly at the black and white border collie. "Barney! Come here, boy!"

Sandra thought, and when I go, I won't hurt the dog.

She hadn't always been that way. She'd been someone who'd had big plans, dreams. It hurt to remember that, but it was also important that she do so. Maybe they were just the same pedestrian dreams that all smart, somewhat indulged girls shared a version of—glamorous travel, success in some arts field, an epic but ultimately doomed love affair—but they had been *hers*. When she had been a person. Sandra thought of them as she cleared away the detritus of their breakfast and loaded the dishwasher after Bastian had left for the office. He had wanted them to get a maid, but as much as she hated cleaning, she hated that idea even more. She imagined herself, the idle housewife, sitting on the sofa watching the maid clean. *What the fuck does she do all day?* she imagined the maid thinking.

What the fuck indeed. She couldn't have said. And Bastian didn't care enough to ask, somewhat fortunately because between the imaginary maid thinking it and Bastian asking it, she would have felt compelled to come up with an answer, and she thought that if she tried to enumerate the substance of her days, or the lack of substance to be more precise, it would all crumble before her, a stark reveal of the utter pointlessness of her existence.

She had an idea that life was like a series of knots tied in a rope. The knots were those critical moments, the ones where you made a choice that substantially sent your life in another direction from the one it was on. You couldn't just undo them, ever. She had once shared this idea with Bastian, when they used to talk about things, but he saw it differently. Bastian was one of those infinite-worlds types, someone who believed that when a butterfly flapped its wings, it could and did change everything. In Bastian's mind, there were countless Bastians, endless universes of new ones created with every breath he drew.

That alone, Sandra thought, ought to have suggested to her their fundamental incompatibility. But it was too late now; that knot had been long since tied.

A line from her life before came to mind: *This is how the world ends, not with a bang but a whimper.*

Did she really want to go out on a whimper?

This was no revelation. She regularly worked her way through these kinds of thoughts. They all ended up in the same place:

*I have to get out of here.*

*Here* was paradise, was everything anyone could want. Luxury. Security. The time and the space to do anything she wanted. God only knew that Bastian would be happy if she found something to do. She could become a great painter, in all that time and space, or a great writer, or a great actress. Maybe she could become a scientist, discover the cure for everything, or save kittens or orphans or stop climate change. Maybe she could run an empire. Maybe she could think of something she might want to do, if the rest of her life wasn't so fucking barren.

She was ungrateful; she knew she was. People would kill—well, maybe not kill, not most people, the true crime podcasts she sometimes listened to notwithstanding, but people would put up with a lot for the opportunity to lead her barren life. It wouldn't be barren for them. Other people knew how to make meaning, and anyway, plenty of people didn't have a fraction of what she did, materially speaking, and dealt with far worse circumstances, and still thrived, or if they didn't thrive, they at least didn't whine about it all the time. Not that Sandra whined to anyone outside of her own head, not that there was anyone to whine to if she did. All of her old friends had fallen away years ago, their lives headed down separate paths, and she'd not been able to make any close ones again since. She was disgusted by her own uselessness, her lack of passion. No wonder Bastian was disgusted by her as well.

*I have to get out of here.*

*Here* was many things: just at the moment, it was less existential than usual and more immediate. She had to get out of the house. She couldn't bear another moment within those walls

Walls that weren't hers. Nothing there was hers. It was all Bastian's. She owned none of it, although a divorce court would say otherwise, but sometimes she fantasised about just walking away, free and clear, leaving all of it behind.

To do that would take courage, and if Sandra had ever had courage—and she believed that once, she had—it had been diminished over the years just like her dreams.

She got a jacket off the hook near the door because it was a cool Pacific Northwest morning, autumn slowly drawing in the days and lengthening the nights. Their drive was a long, sweeping one. Bastian had paid top dollar for their privacy and security, and she let herself out of the gate at the bottom of it. She ought to go downtown, she thought. She could call the car service Bastian had given her the number for. She couldn't remember the last time she'd been there. Maybe she'd go see a movie or just walk through the Park Blocks or down by the waterfront and people watch. Maybe she would even visit some of her old haunts, the places she and Bastian used to go see shows when they were students, like the Crystal Ballroom and the Roseland, or before that even, when she used to hang out at the Satyricon with gutter punks just to piss off her parents. The Satyricon had been gone forever, though, like her parents—like everything in her past—and suddenly even the quiet sidewalk on the eminently civilised street lined with other gates and long winding driveways to unostentatious comfort and tasteful wealth was too much; she felt exposed. Sandra pulled her jacket more tightly round her and walked the few hundred feet back to the gate in quick, focused steps, not looking around her at the expanse of the sky, of the world.

Once on the other side of the gate, she breathed a little easier, but she really didn't feel better until she was back in the house. She hung her jacket up again and remembered that she needed to do some cleaning—it was part of her deal with Bastian, in exchange for not getting the maid. Of course there were multiple Roombas and robotic mops to keep the floors clean, and a man came to wash the windows regularly and another one came to take care of the grounds and someone even came to pick up Barney several times a week and take him to doggie day care. Sandra did her best to avoid interacting with any of them. Sometimes she caught herself remembering the first place she and Bastian had lived together, a place off Hawthorne that they shared with a couple of hippies whose lives revolved around either going to Burning Man or preparing to go to Burning Man. She and Bastian would lie in bed together on their days off and smoke weed and watch terrible comedies, or they would sling some camping gear into Bastian's ancient Volvo and head out of town, or they would go see a band. Bastian had a guitar then, wrote songs sometimes—good ones—but it was tech he really loved, tech that was going to make their fortune. "I'm going to give you everything," he used to say. He never asked her if she wanted him to give her everything. That was back when he had days off. When she thought back on it all, it seemed like someone else's life, something she had seen on TV or in a movie or read in a book.

She made a quick pass through the kitchen, wiping down already-pristine surfaces and rearranging knives and forks in a drawer before heading down the hall, pausing outside Bastian's office—Bluebeard's Den, as she had always called it, because he forbade her to clean in there (forbade was too strong a word, he said don't bother) and left it locked much of the time. Sandra was surprised to see that the door was ajar, but he *had* been in a hurry that morning when he'd finally got ready to leave, coming back twice from the car to get something he'd forgotten.

She pushed the door open, gently.

It wasn't *really* Bluebeard's Den. She'd been in there plenty of times before. His locking it was a kind of habit; when he left it unlocked, it created no angst. Whatever secrets Bastian had—and there was no doubt in her mind that he had plenty—they were not of the analogue sort. He did not need a room to conceal what he wished to keep hidden.

Bastian's office, in fact, could not have been more devoid of personality. If its style had a name, it would be something like Standard Dull; nothing on the walls, a plain desk, a couple of monitors, a brown fake-wood bookcase with a predictable selection of tech and business books displayed. Even the view, in a house that offered spectacular Portland West Hills vistas from nearly every window, was dull, looking out on the driveway and the gate at the bottom.

Sandra went in and sat at his desk, whirled around a few times in the chair until she felt slightly sick. And yet it was a good feeling—it was a *feeling*, something other than shame and self-hatred, an actual sensation, and it reminded her of being a child, lying on her stomach on the stool her mother had in the kitchen and spinning herself round and round and round.

She pulled idly at the drawers, a boring middle drawer with some pens and thumb drives in it, a boring empty upper right-hand drawer, a boring lower right-hand drawer with nothing in it but a thin file that, when she opened it, contained some boring investment paperwork, a boring left-hand drawer—

—that didn't open.

She gave it a yank again, thinking something was stuck and causing it to catch, but it was locked.

You didn't lock something unless you didn't want someone to find out what was in it.

If you were Bastian Dufresne, you didn't lock something unless you didn't want your wife to find out what was in it.

"Oh, Bastian," Sandra said. "How very clumsy of you."

Arguably not as clumsy as it could have been; there was no key in sight in any of the other drawers. He might keep it anywhere, but knowing Bastian, he kept it on his keyring because it was handy and because there was no chance of Sandra spotting it there because he knew she was afraid to drive.

At that moment Barney came springing in, and she shouted at him because Barney wasn't allowed to be in there as Sandra was not (not really), and if he saw signs that Barney was in there he'd know she had been as well, but of course if Bastian had left the door ajar he couldn't expect Barney to leave it unexplored. All the same, Sandra jumped up and then turned back to survey the desk area: how had he left it? Where had his chair been? Would he remember?

"Barney, get out!" Sandra shouted again, and followed her own orders, getting out as well, leaving the door ever so slightly ajar. She'd pretend she hadn't even noticed it if Bastian asked.

*I have to get out of here.*

She was the model wife at dinner (eggplant parmesan, one of her specialties), asking him about his day and feigning interest. She saw how it flattered him and swallowed something that felt like contempt, which she could ill afford because it was difficult to conceal. She didn't want to appear too unlike her usual self, so after she cleared up the table she said she was going to take a bath. She usually took a novel with her, some indifferent thriller, but this time, instead of reading, she lay there among the suds and thought.

Bastian was an early-to-bed and early-to-rise sort. She tended to follow his schedule because it wasn't as though she had anything better to do, but unlike him, she was not a sound sleeper. After they went to bed, she waited until his breathing was deep and even and then got up. In the kitchen, she got herself a glass of water to use as an excuse, although the chances Bastian would wake up and ask her what she was doing were nil. He never woke up. Without fail, he slept the sleep of the utterly blameless, the unconcerned.

Bless him for his predictable ways. He always hung his coat on the rack just inside the door, and his keys were always in his coat pocket.

Sandra retrieved them and crept up the hall. There were several keys on the ring, but she knew which one went to the office—there had never been any reason to hide it—and she let herself in easily. And then to the desk, where she switched on the lamp next to the window. Two of the mystery keys on the ring were obviously too large; there were three others—to what? what did he need these small secretive keys for?—and she tried each of them, hardly daring to breathe when the second one threatened to stick in the lock and not come out. Third time was the charm; the key slid neatly in the lock, the lock turned and she opened the drawer.

She had not thought what she would find in there—she had not let herself think, but now that she did, staring at a wooden box, she couldn't really imagine. *Not another key*, that was all she *could* imagine, a scavenger hunt into infinity for more boxes and more keys, but no, it opened without the need of a key, and she peered within.

The box held a hank of long red-gold hair, tied into three knots.

Sandra instinctively touched her own head; she had not had long hair or red-gold hair for many years, but it was unmistakably her own.

For a fleeting moment, she was touched at the idea of Bastian saving a lock of her hair, *how romantic*, but that quickly turned into *but also creepy*.

She touched the hair then as she had her head, and each of the three knots. *Why knots? Why three of them?*

There was nothing else in the drawer. This was the single thing he meant to conceal. That had to mean it was important.

And where had he got it from? She touched her own head a second time. Surely she would remember an occasion when her husband put scissors to her head and chopped off a considerable chunk of it.

But maybe not. Hadn't he done the honours himself a few times back when they were broke? Once she'd ended up with ragged bangs she'd had to pin back with barrettes for weeks. And there had been the time she'd cut it all off—or Bastian had, rather. "Look at this," he'd said, pointing at a picture of a woman online. "You'd look great with your hair like that." She hadn't thought so. She'd liked her long locks, but Bastian said it would look nice so she went along with it. She'd felt a little bit ill as he'd made the first cuts and the swathes of hair hit the floor, and by then it was too late to stop it. She'd worn her hair no longer than shoulder length ever since because it was easier to care for and because Bastian liked it that way, or she guessed he did.

How had she forgotten that?

She'd learned to trim it herself, of course. She hadn't set foot in an expensive salon in years.

Sandra ran her hands over the knots again. They weren't like the tangled cords. They were tied deliberately, and at even intervals.

She forgot to be quiet, and slammed the drawer shut, locking it quickly, then turned off the light and got out of the room, another lock, and back to Bastian's coat and—right hand pocket? Left hand pocket? She couldn't remember; she thrust them in one, and then went in the kitchen and sat at one of the stools beside the gleaming marble island.

It was in those moments that she started to know things she had been aware of all along. Things she had not allowed herself to fully understand.

"I couldn't sleep," she said to him by way of explanation when he came bleary-eyed into the kitchen that morning, a questioning look on his face.

He opened the refrigerator and bent over to poke through its contents so she couldn't see his face, but he couldn't disguise the fact that his next question didn't sound as idle as he clearly wanted it to: "What did you do?"

"Nothing. Watched something. Read."

He stood up, looking at her over the top of the refrigerator door. "So which was it? Nothing? Watched something? Or read?"

"Oh, you know." She slid off the stool.

"What did you watch?"

"Some . . . thing." She waved her hand in the general direction of the living room.

"You didn't jump ahead in *Succession* without me, did you?"

She laughed. It sounded fake even to her. "Of course not."

She thought then that he couldn't ask again what she had done, or watched; it would be too strange, but she had underestimated him. Strange to who, after all? What would she do, who would she tell?

So over breakfast, he asked again: "What did you watch?"

"Nothing."

"You said you watched something."

"I know. I—"

"Sandra," he said, "are you lying to me?"

It wasn't like him to be so direct, and she didn't have to fake her shock. "No! Of course not. Why would I lie about whether I watched something?"

He didn't answer and finished eating his yogurt, then announced, "I'm going to work from home today." That was unusual. Even during the worst of the pandemic, he had gone into the office most days.

Sandra loaded the dishwasher. She tried to remember when she had started to be afraid to leave the house. But long before that, she had dropped out of school. And she had started to lose her friends when she and Bastian had become so closed in—or rather, she had; he still did things, had a life outside. She had always thought of it as something that happened fairly recently. It was a passing thing, something she would get over. That was what she told herself at first. The days and weeks and months and years had blurred together when she tried to think back across them.

*How long has it been, Sandra?*

She had hoped to have a child once—children, she wanted more than one—but she remembered thinking she couldn't bring them into a world with such a frightened mother. So when she got over her fear—soon, she would deal with it soon—she and Bastian could have them.

*How long?*

It was remarkable, really, how twenty years could pass in a flash. One minute you were young and you had your whole life ahead of you. There was time for everything. And in the next, all those possibilities had passed you by.

Sandra picked up the ethernet cable she'd untangled the day before. It was twisted into knots again.

She typed on her phone, "why do cords tangle by themselves".

There were articles about principles of physics, cord lengths, and "agitation", but as far as Sandra could see, nobody really knew why or how it happened. It reminded her of an article she'd read once that said physicists were baffled about how bicycles actually worked, what physical laws kept you upright and moving forward. The world was full of so many simple, unknowable things.

Sandra remembered the first time she'd seen Bastian walking across campus. It always sounded like she was making it up, but he'd stepped out from behind a tree into a ray of watery spring sunshine, and it was like he was some angelic, otherworldly creature. Of course, he wasn't—he had parents and an older brother, and embarrassing yearbook photos just like everyone else. But in the moment, seeing him in his rumpled Everclear t-shirt and jeans—he was never dishevelled any longer—and his fair hair, casually shoulder-length, she thought *Who* is *that boy?* and in the next moment she had a gut-level certainty that their fates were entwined. It was the kind of thing her friend Erica would say; Erica who used to put her faith in tarot cards and astrological occurrences and synchronicity, unlike the staunchly materialist Sandra . . . and yet. And yet.

Why had she not taken her lock of hair when she had the chance? She didn't care any longer that it would raise the stakes, that he would then know. It would force the confrontation that had been too long in coming. *Why were you in my office*, he would say, and she would thrust it at him, demand to know why it was there, what it all meant. Only it wouldn't happen that way either. It would all be more strategic than that, each of them waiting in bated silences for the other to crack.

She could lie awake until Bastian was asleep again, creep out of bed once more and let herself in, but she had the feeling he was already onto her, that the keys would no longer be in their usual reliable place. But she couldn't go on in this way. She had to get to it. Wild thoughts assailed her: she would burn the house down, she would batter the door open and then fake a burglary.

The answer, of course, came to her in a much more prosaic way, via a subreddit created for—who else?—hobbyist lockpickers, along with a vast library of YouTube videos.

Bastian worked from home all week, and Sandra did her best to behave as though nothing was out of the ordinary. Everything was though, of course, and not just because of her discovery. It was strange to have him there all day. She found herself making up tasks to do, or to pretend to do, wondering what exactly it was she occupied herself with all day when he was out. She was pretty sure she didn't sit, hands folded at the dining room table until it was time to get dinner started; but when she tried to think back on her days, they just seemed like a grey stretch of sameness.

She didn't know why she bothered, really, because it wasn't as though Bastian paid attention to what she was doing. She could hear him in there, making Zoom calls, laughing loudly sometimes—she couldn't remember the last time he'd laughed like that in her presence, unless it was something that Barney did—and at other times quiet, doing what she knew he called his "deep work". She spent a lot of time reading the subreddit, but she felt like she had to have something else to hand to pretend to be working on in case he came in, which he never did. There were various projects lying around that she'd abandoned and used now as decoys: some crocheting, some watercolours, some books recommended by Reese's and Oprah's book clubs that never held her attention. She'd crochet a few rows and look at her phone, rinse and repeat. She wished she could just order one of the many lockpicking kits online, but every purchase would have to go through an account of Bastian's, and he pored over each statement every month as though trying to uncover evidence that she'd been doing a little money laundering in her spare time. But she was still a quick learner, and she'd been handy with tools, once. It had been her dad's hobby: fixing things, woodworking, endless home improvements, and she'd always been his eager helper.

She read the forum and she looked at videos and she thought she had the hang of it. She tested it, in other parts of the house. She handily popped open one of the bathroom doors and the door to one of the guest rooms (they never had guests) using, respectively, a credit card and a hairpin. She was reasonably confident, but not so confident that it was something she planned to undertake in the middle of the night, and anyway, once she had what she was after, she knew what came next.

*I have to get out of here.*

The first time she'd tried to leave him was before they were even married. She had looked around and noticed the way their life had changed, that they were turning into people she didn't know any longer. Bastian was already a rising tech star, and they went to dinners and parties and happy hours where everyone laughed a little too loudly and drank too much, and on one of those nights she found herself standing on a balcony; she couldn't even remember where they were, but she was out there alone, looking across the lights of the city below, and she felt a presence beside her. "Sometimes I fantasise about throwing a bomb down into the middle of it all," a woman's voice said, and Sandra turned to see someone she'd been introduced to earlier standing there but she couldn't remember the woman's name—Lindy? Louisa? Leila? The woman was older than her and a little brusque. Sandra liked her.

"I think about flying," she said. "Soaring over all those lights and up above the clouds to where it's just all dark and quiet. On the edge of space."

The woman blinked, but she didn't seem especially disturbed or surprised. She had a cigarette in one hand and a cocktail in the other and she leaned her elbows on the balcony, blowing smoke rings. "My advice?" she said. "Do it."

Sandra laughed. "Right now?"

But the woman was serious. "Get out now," she said. "You don't want to get yourself tangled up with this crew. If you're lucky, you'll be a starter wife."

"And if I'm not?"

"You'll end up like me," the woman said, and barked. She didn't really bark, but her laugh sounded like one, mirthless and desperate.

It had been such a brief exchange, but it was as though it had unlocked all the inchoate doubts that had been plaguing Sandra for months. Later that evening she felt something uncoil in her stomach, something like joy, or maybe possibility—weren't they the same thing?

*You can just leave him.*

She could. There was nothing to bind her; she could walk out the next day, or that very night if she felt like it. She hadn't spoken to any of her old friends for a while, but not for so long that she couldn't turn up at Erica's or Amy's or she could even go to her parents—that was trickier, there would be harder questions, but the point was there was nothing keeping her.

And yet she hadn't gone. Bastian had talked so much on the way back from the party that she couldn't think, and then she had a headache, and when she got up the next day, after sleeping all morning, she felt heavy and feverish. She'd barely had anything to drink at the party; it wasn't a hangover. But all the resolve had drained out of her. The woman might as well have suggested to her that she really could fly.

It was the following week before Bastian was out of the house again. That was almost unheard of, not just the days of working from home, but not going anywhere in the evenings or on the weekend either. Normally he kept a full schedule of work-related social engagements, plus there was the gym and the various boards that he sat on. He didn't even head out for a run. In every other way, he behaved perfectly ordinarily, but as each day passed, she had the sense that her time was short, although she couldn't have said what that meant.

On that Monday it was raining, and she watched him back the car out of the carport and turn it around. She made herself wait twenty minutes—surely he was at the office by then—before she went to work. The door was a basic pin tumbler lock, just as the internet had promised her it would probably be, and she made short work of it. The desk drawer was, surprisingly, a little more challenging, but she persisted with the help of a paperclip and YouTube, and less than an hour after Bastian had left, she was sliding the drawer out again. There was the box. She opened it.

There was nothing inside.

In disbelief, she scrabbled at it as though the hank of hair would somehow materialise. She felt all along the inside of the drawer as well, even though she could see with her own eyes that it was empty. Of course. Of course he had known. Of course he had taken it. She had shown her hand too easily. And if he had now shown his as well, what did it matter?

Sandra pushed the drawer shut. She supposed she had to relock it now, which hadn't occurred to her before. She picked up her phone again to look up whether this was possible and put it down again.

How had she been so stupid? A rookie mistake—hadn't she read enough thrillers to have anticipated this? If he hadn't figured it out from her strange behaviour in the kitchen that morning after her discovery—and Bastian had always said, and repeatedly proved, that she was an open book to him—then the tracker he had doubtless installed on her phone left him with no doubts. She didn't know how to look for it, but she knew it was there.

Barney was barking. Was Bastian back home again already? Sandra leapt up from the desk and across the room, pulling the door shut behind her. She was in the kitchen loading the dishwasher when he came in.

"Forgot my phone," he said as he breezed across the kitchen, grabbed it from where it sat on the counter—in her haste to get into his office she hadn't seen it at all—and then he was out the door again and gone.

She stood there in the kitchen for a long time after he left. She had expected them to go through some kind of ludicrous choreography, each of them pretending not to know what the other was up to. Him checking on the office. Her, casual: *I don't know. Guess you didn't lock it.* But none of those things had happened. It seemed like he had genuinely just forgotten his phone and innocently come back for it.

The first tiny swells of self-doubt began to crest.

*I have to get out of here.*

Sandra put on her boots and her hooded rain jacket. She walked down the driveway again, passed through the gate again. Today the sky was low and oppressive. It was raining. *Today I will walk farther than I did last time.* She did, but only just. By the time she turned around she felt like something heavy was pressing on her chest, squeezing the breath out of her. It was something of a relief to return—home—the word sounded loathsome in her head.

She had dreamed about seeing the world once. She had imagined herself an adventuress. She was going to do it all: take a boat down the Amazon, fall asleep under Moroccan skies, walk the Great Wall of China. That had been the impetus for her second effort to leave Bastian, in fact. She remembered thinking if she could just get a little space, a little time away. She had found a language school in Mexico, an immersion program. Her Spanish had been good once—she'd minored in it in college—but she hadn't kept it up. Bastian was so busy at work. The break would be good for them both, she'd thought. She had gathered all the information on it that she could. Later she'd realised that she'd been so meticulous in her planning because nailing down every little detail took up time, delayed raising the idea with Bastian, which she finally did after dinner one night, in the manner of someone presenting a proposal to a sceptical supervisor. She had talked for a long time before she realised that he hadn't said anything, and stopped mid-sentence.

He said, "Go on. It sounds very interesting."

But she didn't have anything more to say, hadn't for a few minutes, at least.

She could no longer remember what she had expected from him, except that it would be some kind of resistance, so she felt almost deflated when he said, "It would be a good opportunity for you, wouldn't it? Why don't you put some dates together and we can take another look at it?"

She remembered that she had felt buoyant. *I'm doing something. I'm really doing something. I'm becoming myself again.* She barely let herself glance at the idea underneath it: *I won't come back.* Away from Bastian, from the life they shared together (from his life, that he shared with her), she would shore up the resolve that she needed. She continued doing research that evening on her laptop, looking up places she wanted to visit, pulling her old Spanish books off the shelves and letting the language roll around on her tongue again, excavating old longings that felt almost atavistic in their purity and intensity.

But her dreams that night were terrifying ones: of walking on a road, lost and afraid, a stranger in a strange land, and something at her heels that she could never quite see or name that threatened to devour her. She woke up with a sense of incalculable loss.

She never mentioned the plan to Bastian again, although he brought it up a few times and she demurred. It had all become unimaginable to her, and now she couldn't remember the last time she'd been more than a few steps from her house, when she had stopped accompanying Bastian to the parties and dinners and happy hours. Had he stopped inviting her, or had she stopped accepting? She must be an embarrassment to him, his colleagues must think of her as some kind of madwoman. You weren't supposed to talk about people like that anymore. You were supposed to talk about therapies and illnesses and medications, but she felt she was quite mad, like a woman in a gothic story, the wife hidden in the attic, locked in an asylum. She didn't belong to their world. She never had.

What she was imagining now—it was crazy, it was right up there with people who think their loved ones have been replaced by doubles or something equally delusional. Maybe she did want to leave Bastian, but it wasn't because he was some sinister, controlling, spying monster. Maybe he wasn't the most sensitive or attentive, but he had never been anything but supportive of her.

A few years ago he'd shown her *Blade Runner*. She'd never seen it, never been a sci-fi fan but was vaguely aware it was one of those movies that seemed really significant to some people. Afterwards, she couldn't stop thinking about the character of Rachael, the replicant who had no idea what she was. All her memories, everything about her, had been invented. *I could be one of those.* Bastian might have made her, created her out of some strange impoverished idea of what a woman was. She knew it was mere fancy. She knew she was real. All of her memories were visceral and true, but Rachael had probably believed that as well.

Sandra couldn't remember the third time she'd tried to leave Bastian, but she knew there'd been a third time.

That night, she dreamed.

Sandra hadn't dreamed for a long time. Whenever she mentioned this fact to Bastian, he said, "Of course, you do, everyone dreams. Every *thing* dreams. You just don't remember them."

But she was sure he was wrong, sure that for many years now, sleep for her had been a featureless void. She had once imagined there was a mansion with hundreds—no, *thousands* of rooms—and in each of those rooms was one of her undreamt dreams. That night she found it, at the top of a sweeping driveway that was very like the one she lived at the top of now. The mansion was so enormous that when she looked up, its highest storeys vanished into the night sky. The front door was a massive, wooden, medieval thing, and she thought it would never open, but the moment she put her hand to it, of course it did, because it was hers.

On the other side of the door, in a kind of foyer, was a spiral staircase. She began climbing it, but she didn't stop on the first or the second or even the fourteenth or fortieth floor. She climbed and she climbed. Some of the floors she passed were quiet, but others were bedlam: dreams shrieking and howling at their doorways to get out. The air grew thin. She paused at last, having climbed thousands of stairs past hundreds of floors. Before her was a small red door with a crystal doorknob. She turned it and pushed the door open.

At first, there was nothing but darkness on the other side, but then her eyes began to adjust. The room was a small one, perhaps eight by eight feet. It appeared to be entirely empty. She had a brief flash of lucidity: *is the message that there is*

*nothing, that I am nothing, that there are no dreams after all*
before her unconscious reasserted itself. A sliver of new moon
appeared in the window, casting a sliver of light across rough
wooden floorboards; then the moon waxed, growing larger
and fuller and brighter, and the walls of the room were blood
red, and they were pulsing, and the house was alive and she
was at its beating heart.

She was thrust out into the cacophony of Bastian's hateful
alarm, lying on her back on the floor, slick with sweat and
exhausted from climbing the stairs.

But, no, there had been no stairs, not really, only there
had been, and Bastian was rolling over in the bed and staring
at her.

"What the hell are you doing?"

"Stretching," she said, and it was all so absurd she started
laughing, real laughter, rolling up from deep within, she was
crying and she was laughing and finally she pulled herself
together.

But Bastian was already gone, and she heard the sound
of the shower from the bathroom. She lifted each of her legs,
experimentally, but the dream-exhaustion had dissipated,
and she was slightly disappointed as she got to her feet and
made her way without effort downstairs to the kitchen. *It was
real. It wasn't just a dream.* Barney came running in and she
tousled his ears and put his food down, but she wasn't *there*:
she was still in the house, still in the room. All Bastian said
when he came in was, "Some night then, eh?" with what she
had once thought of as an adorable quirk, the single raised
eyebrow, and they ate breakfast just like everything was
normal, Bastian already replying to messages on his phone
and saying don't bother with dinner, it was going to be a late

night, and she said, "What are you doing?" and he looked at her, surprised she'd asked, and answered, "Just a dinner. Some investors," and she said, "I could come."

That got his attention. "What?"

"I could come."

"Why—it's a business dinner, why would you want to come?"

"I used to come to your business dinners a lot."

"And you said—" he raised an index finger, as if to stop her speaking even though she wasn't trying to—"you said they were interminable and you'd rather be flayed alive than ever sit through another one."

"I exaggerated."

She expected him to protest further, but he shrugged. "Suit yourself. I'll send a car to pick you up at six. I gotta go, early meeting this morning."

With him out of the house, she began packing. Once she started, she was shocked to realise how little she wanted to take away with her, how few of the things she ostensibly owned felt like hers. She pushed away the picture of herself making it to the bottom of the driveway and turning back. The dinner tonight would be her entry back into the world. She would remember how to talk to people, how to not feel so exposed, like she might be swallowed up. That would give her the courage she needed. Tomorrow she would leave for good.

It was while digging through her jewellery box, something she never touched, that she found it. She had as much right to the money in their joint accounts as Bastian did, but in case he cut her off, she would need access to funds, at least temporarily, and she thought she could sell some of the valuable pieces to tide her over until she'd got somewhere far away and found a lawyer. The jewellery box was something her parents had given her in the early days after she and

Bastian were married, and it had a false bottom, a touching, irrelevant gesture. Bastian had laughed at it later. "The last line of defence against home invasion!" he said. She hadn't liked him laughing—she remembered the pensive look on her father's face, almost as though he thought Bastian was stealing her away from them—but she laughed, too, because they were supposed to be a team now. Secretly, though, she had used the false bottom because it had been important to her parents.

What she expected to find in there, she had—the really pricey stuff was locked up in a safe deposit box although she'd held onto a pair of diamond earrings, an emerald bracelet, a string of pearls—but there was something else.

Sandra unfolded the slip of paper under the jewellery.

It was in her own handwriting, though she had no recollection of writing it:

*He has been in the red heart of the house and he has hidden something there. You won't remember this. You won't remember how he knotted and twisted and tangled the threads of time to snare you but you will know that you are unsettled and that something is wrong and you will be right. I can't write it here because it is only in the language of dreams. And I am already forgetting as I write this. I have to hide this now before I've forgotten completely.*

Sandra wasn't sure how long she sat there with the note in her hand. She did not want to put it back lest she forget it again, and who knew how long it would be before she discovered it once more? This might not be the first time she had found it, for that matter. She wished the note had a date on it. She wished it had explained how she had come by the knowledge that led her to write it. But of course, there had probably not been time. She wanted to keep the note with her always, in case she forgot it, but what if she lost it? She would copy it. She would put the copy in the jewellery box and keep the other. It was not lost on her that she might have hatched this exact plan before, but what else could she do?

Once it came to her, she had to work quickly. She found some paper and a pen and when she sat down with it, wondered what she had intended to write. She opened her left hand with the note in it and remembered. She jotted it down as fast as she could. Now why had she done that? What was she supposed to do with it? *Jewellery box*. She had just set it back into the false drawer when her phone rang, Bastian's name blinking on the screen.

"Hey, Sandra, babe, it's a real shit show here." He was on a speaker.

"What?" she said. She couldn't remember the last time he'd called her *babe*, if ever.

"The dinner meeting tonight. There's been a crisis and—well, it's better if you don't come."

"But I want to."

A beat, then a long sigh. "Sandra, you can't. We're going to be talking about intellectual property, stuff we can't discuss with outsiders. People not in the company, I mean. It would be like you following me to work and sitting in the office with me."

"Okay."

"Sorry. I know you're disappointed. I'll make it up to you this weekend, maybe we'll go somewhere?" He said it casually, like it hadn't been months, years, since they'd done that very thing.

"Sure."

She sat there holding the phone in one hand, a crumpled piece of paper in the other. *What's in my hand?* She made to throw it in a nearby wastebasket, but glanced at it just before she did so; read it again, remembered it again.

*Bastian, what have you done to me?*

✳

The third time she tried to leave him it had been real. There had been no daydreaming about it beforehand, no you-go-girl delusions of self-actualisation. There had been fury: slamming doors and drawers, slamming her suitcase open on their bed, slamming clothes into it without looking at them. Bastian had come in.

"What are you doing?"

"What does it look like I'm doing?"

He had watched her for a few minutes. She'd banged the suitcase closed and yanked it off the bed.

"You need to calm down."

She couldn't answer him. She imagined that if she opened her mouth, what would spill out would not be words but something foul and poisonous.

He grabbed her arms when she tried to push past him. The suitcase hit her leg, and hurt—later a beautiful bruise would bloom there.

She found her words. "Let me go."

"No."

She couldn't believe she'd heard him, or that he was really restraining her. *We are not these kinds of people.*

"You're hurting me."

He shoved her then, back into the room, and she stumbled but didn't fall. The door slammed. Bastian was on the other side of it. She flew at the door, twisting the knob, hammering on it, but it wouldn't budge. She could hear herself screaming at him like she was somebody else. "Have you locked me in? *Have you fucking locked me in? I'll kill you!*"

It was the last three words that did it, words that brought her back to her senses. She thrust her hands into her hair, pulled hard until her scalp ached as she tried to get control of her ragged breath. She sat down on the edge of the bed and tried to think it all through, what had brought her to this moment, but the more she thought about it, the more confused she felt.

She dug into her pocket for a tissue and instead pulled out a piece of paper that had her writing on it, but she didn't remember writing what she read there:

*He has been in the red heart of the house . . .*

After Bastian's phone call telling her she couldn't join him for dinner, Sandra slept for a while. She was so exhausted. She woke unrefreshed and disoriented, unsure whether it was night or day or where she was. For a moment she thought she was in her childhood bedroom. Then she turned her head on the pillow and felt something stuck to her cheek—a piece of paper?

Sandra read it again.

*Where is the heart of the house?*

Sandra got out of bed and took a shower. Going from the shower to the bedroom in her robe, she froze at the sound of people downstairs in the kitchen, then she heard Barney's nails skittering on the floor. Of course. Doggie day care bringing him home. Sandra told herself to focus. She dressed quickly and as nondescriptly as she could: jeans and a black t-shirt. She got the suitcase out again and threw a few more articles of clothing into it. She picked up her phone and started to scroll for the car service, then stopped and put it down. There was a landline downstairs in the kitchen. She used it to call a cab company. A taxi would be at the bottom of the driveway in an hour. It was too long. Couldn't they come sooner? They'd try. *I'll be there waiting*, she told them. She shut the door to the kitchen so Barney would stay in there, then sat for a while with her suitcase just inside the front door, formulating a plan.

The bus station—that was the way to go. She'd take out as much cash as she could and she'd get a ticket for whatever bus was leaving next. She thought about movie montages where people somehow manage to cut and dye their hair in public restrooms. She thought, it's hard enough to just wash your hands in a public restroom. She put on her rain jacket with the hood. It would have to do to disguise her features. She imagined Bastian interrogating the taxi driver. She would have him take her somewhere else, maybe the airport, and she'd double back to the bus station on the light rail. And she'd get off the bus before the destination she'd bought a ticket for, and she'd do the same thing again at the next place and the next. She could visualise it all, this time a different movie, a map unfurling onscreen, showing the zig-zag points of her journey across the country. For some reason, it was in black and white, and the thrilling escape music that accompanied it was tinny and old-fashioned as well. Sandra watched the minute hand on the grandfather clock in the foyer crawl forward. It occurred to her to take out her phone and leave it on the table there. She needed to go down to the bottom of the drive in case the taxi was early. She picked up her suitcase and put it back down.

*I have to get out of here.*

She picked up the suitcase again, but it was no use.

Sandra sat down again and watched the minute hand crawl past the hour mark, when the cab company had said someone would be arriving. She heard the phone ringing in the kitchen, probably the company asking where she was. She imagined the driver sitting down at the bottom of the drive, cursing the stupid crazy rich lady who had wasted his time, calling him out for nothing, losing him money.

He was so close. He was just down the hill. She could run, and she might make it before he peeled away in anger. She didn't need the suitcase, not really. She could run and it would be over in minutes, before she knew it she would be in his car and away they would go, winding down through the West Hills, past Washington Park and into downtown, past Pioneer Square to the waterfront, the bridges and across the Willamette River—she could picture the journey almost as though it was already happening even though it had been so long since she'd seen any of those places.

Five minutes, ten minutes, fifteen minutes, he wouldn't be there any longer. Her window for escape had opened and closed.

She had something in her hand. She looked at it.

*He has been in the red heart of the house . . .*

Sandra thought, the problem is that this house has no heart. This house is an ice-cold dame in a film noir. This house is brutalist architecture without the architecture. This house would cut you to ribbons soon as look at you.

It was nothing like *her* house, the one she had dreamed.

*He has hidden something in* your *heart.*

She was still sitting on her suitcase in the foyer. It was getting darker inside and out. She wasn't sure what time it was and she could no longer read the hands on the face of the grandfather clock, but she didn't want to turn on a light. That felt like defeat. As long as she sat there in the growing dark, she could believe that in a moment, she was going to get up, put her hand on the doorknob, turn it and walk outside.

*How do things get so tangled up?*

She wished she could go back to Sandra on campus that day she saw him for the first time and whisper in her ear. *Turn away. Forget that boy.* But Bastian-then hadn't been Bastian-now, had he? Of course he had. You didn't just turn out to be a certain way unless that person had been inside you all along.

*What does that say about me?*

She must have sat for hours, because the next thing she was aware of was the sound of Bastian's car coming up the drive. She jumped up; the suitcase fell over and banged on the floor and Barney started barking in the kitchen.

She heard Bastian coming into the kitchen from the garage, Barney making the bark-whine sounds he did every time his master came home. And Bastian's voice. "Hey boy! What are you doing stuck in here?" And then, "Sandra?"

She waited for him. He pushed open the kitchen door. Barney scrambled out and stood barking at her like she was an intruder.

Bastian snapped on the hall light. "Sandra? What are you doing?"

She stood there feeling like a naughty child.

She said, "I can leave. You can't stop me from leaving."

"What are you talking about?" His face was so aghast she could almost believe he was as shocked as he pretended to be.

"I'm going," she said, but she didn't move.

"Going where?" His voice was very even.

"Away from here."

"Sandra, what is this about?"

She couldn't remember what it was about. She only knew that she had to go, in the way that you might know that you needed food or water when you were starving or dying of thirst.

"Where is the heart of the house?" she asked him.

"What?"

She kicked the suitcase hard and was pleased that, ineffectual as it was, it made him jump. "Where is the heart of the house? The red room? What did you hide there?" The words tumbled out of her, she didn't understand why she was saying them or what they meant.

"You can leave anytime you like, stop talking to me like I'm keeping you prisoner." He was getting angry. "Go, Sandra. The door's right there in front of you." *See how far you get*, he didn't have to finish it.

She pictured it: the road, dark now, rising up before her from the bottom of the drive, a knot of streets to navigate until she reached a part of the city where there were cabs. It would be miles to walk. She might get lost. She might get hit by a car, invisible in her drab clothes that were meant to help her blend in.

She said, "This house isn't real. None of this is real."

As she spoke, she had the sense of a wave rolling beneath them, and then a sudden, sharp jolt, then another. Barney started barking again. The table she'd set her phone on fell over and her phone clattered to the floor. Sandra grabbed for the wall to steady herself. The grandfather clock swayed alarmingly. The house was a ship and they were helpless on an angry ocean. Bastian's car alarm sounded. The grandfather clock smashed to the floor.

The quake was over in seconds. But now there was a second shock, more violent than the first, and she couldn't stay on her feet. A jagged crack split the wall beside her. Somewhere in the house, glass shattered. Other, distant alarms sounded, and then their home alarm, shrieking. Barney howled. When the shaking stopped, she got to her feet and staggered toward the door.

Bastian shouted, "Don't go outside!"

She hesitated for a moment because he was right, after all. It was what she had been taught all her life, you stayed indoors until an earthquake was over, but she pulled the door open and Barney shot past her and she ran, halfway down the drive until the third shock hit and she fell again.

Bastian grabbed her arms from behind. "You idiot," he said. "You stupid fool." His cold fury frightened her. "What did you do?" he demanded. "This is all *your* fault. *You* did this."

Sandra couldn't speak.

"I did everything for you," Bastian snarled. She was afraid to look at him, afraid of what his face would look like. She let herself go limp in his grip, but he didn't let go.

"You're hurting me."

That didn't have any effect either, but what happened next did: there was an enormous boom behind them, an explosive sound like the loudest thunder she'd ever heard.

Bastian released his grip, and turned to look behind them.

The house was collapsing in on itself—but not down, it was moving *upwards*, folding into itself, first the ground floor and then the upper one, suspended in space amid a great howling wind, and debris flew into her face, grit into her eyes so she had to close them, rubbing them with her fists, and then turning fully and watching through her fingers as the house roared and bayed and compacted into a fat, violently twisting cable, so long it disappeared into the sky above and so many knots in it, *how many chances, how many lives*, and the sky was no longer dark but red, fully afire, and with another great thunderous clap, the cable itself vanished in a blinding blaze of crimson.

When Sandra closed her eyes, that crimson was still all she could see, and she was vaguely aware that a dog was barking and howling and a man was screaming and sobbing, but she couldn't take any of it in. She felt thoroughly exposed, as in all the nightmares she'd had about leaving, as though she had been flayed.

Eventually the noises in her immediate vicinity subsided, though there was still chaos elsewhere, distant shouting and still more alarms. It hadn't been the Big One, presumably, because they were still alive, but it had been *a* Big One.

She had rolled herself into a ball, but now, she slowly uncoiled. The air was sulphurous. "Gas explosion," she said to no one. Somewhere farther down the driveway she saw a man and a dog, and she remembered that their names were Bastian and Barney. She got to her feet tentatively and made her way down to them.

"Gas explosion," she said again, and the man—Bastian— turned to her. There was something about his eyes that scared her.

She spoke as if by rote. "Insurance will cover it," she said, and thought, *Shock, that's it, we're all in shock*, weren't they supposed to wrap themselves in those crinkly aluminium blanket things at times like this? She felt her pockets for her phone to call 911 but there was no point in that, was there, the whole city was calling 911 right this very second and it wasn't as though they needed immediate assistance, they weren't injured.

Anyway, there was nothing in her pocket but a crumpled piece of paper. Sandra let it flutter to the ground as she went up to her husband.

He was holding something in his hand, a length of rope. The dog's leash?

"Hey," she said. "We're all together. We made it. That's all that matters."

He was frantically knotting the rope.

"What are you doing?" she said.

"Nothing," he said. "Look," and pointed.

She turned. They were so lucky, she thought. So many people would have lost so much and what great good fortune—their house still stood. The city would be in shock and mourning. There would be so much work to do. Maybe she could do some of it, help out somewhere, make herself useful—but not right away. For now she wanted to be close to home. For now she wanted to stay where she felt secure.

Bastian rested his hand at the small of her back. "We're going to be okay," he said.

Sandra flinched at his touch. A momentary disquiet passed through her and was gone.

# The Vestige

Davavid woke as he was roughly jarred in his bunk. Halfway between sleep and wakefulness, he cried out, and was surprised when a soothing female voice, heavily accented, replied in English. "They are just moving us to a different set of rail gauges," she said. "They are going to pick us up with the crane now."

Gauges—the rail—he was slowly coming back to himself. He was on a night train out of Bucharest to Chișinău and he must be at the border, because he'd read about this, how, car by car, they would actually be picked up and deposited on a separate set of gauges.

The voice said, "It is for defence, you know. From Soviet times." And he said, "How did you know I speak English?"

"You woke up once and you said, 'What's happening?' That—what is it you say? That let the cat out of the bag, right?"

He smiled at her even though the light in the sleeping compartment was too dim for her to see him, and rolled onto his stomach to gaze at the sullen debris of the rail yard, and the grey pre-dawn sky raked by bare winter branches. Through the night, he had imagined that he wasn't sleeping at all, as the heater blasted stifling hot air, leaving his lips and skin and eyes parched. But now he remembered stirring out of fitful dreams once, when someone came in, and claimed the opposite bunk. He'd felt briefly disappointed before falling asleep again; he'd been lucky to get a compartment to himself and he hated the idea of sleeping with a stranger

106

so close, and the inevitable awkwardness that would ensue in the morning, when they couldn't communicate. It hadn't occurred to him for some reason that it would be a girl, which changed everything. Although he didn't actually know what she looked like, she *sounded* attractive.

"I'm Anna," she said, and stuck an arm out across the gap between them. He reached out as well. Her grip was surprisingly firm. "You're American, right?"

"Anna," he said. "That's my cousin's middle name. The one I'm visiting. She used to call herself that sometimes when we were teenagers."

She said, "I don't care what your cousin is named. What is *your* name?"

"David," he said. "How'd you know I'm American? The air of general cluelessness, right?" She laughed. He had made her laugh. That was good. He wasn't used to being the kind of guy who made attractive girls laugh. He could tell she was rummaging around for something and then her face bloomed pale and ghostly above a flashlight. "This is me," she said. He'd already made a picture of her in his mind, and the face before him didn't match it—and why would it? She was less conventionally pretty than the Anna he'd conjured up. On the other hand, her features were more interesting, and suddenly the imagined-Anna couldn't quite hold her own before her flesh-and-blood counterpart and disintegrated with less than a whimper. The girl across from him had dark hair and wide eyes, a strong nose and chin, and an interesting scar above her left eyebrow which, like its right twin, was resolutely unplucked. As she grew older, he thought, she would be what people used to call a "handsome woman".

He said, "Let's turn the lights on."

"No, it's more fun like this. Like secrets. Here. Now you." She passed the flashlight across to him. He had the absurd sensation that he was auditioning for something.

"Ooh," she said. "You are very handsome. This is good news for me, I think."

He was a little taken aback, even though he'd heard somewhere that European girls could be more forward than American ones.

"Oh!" she said. "Listen!" He did, but he couldn't hear anything. "Now we must turn the light on. They are coming to check our passports." She was rummaging in her bag again, and he reached over by the door and fumbled for the light. They blinked at each other in its dull incandescence, at the drab fake wood paneling of the train car, the worn and not-quite-clean look of things. He said, "You were right about not turning the light on," and rummaged for his own passport.

But it wasn't in the pocket of his backpack where he knew he'd stashed it; it didn't seem to be anywhere else, either, he quickly established, checking his bunk, the floor around him, digging into the bag itself and pulling out fistfuls of socks and t-shirts and underwear.

"It's gone," he said, "someone's taken it." Someone had come in while he, or they, were sleeping and taken his passport. But who would do that? Who would know he had a passport worth taking? Had someone overheard him buying his ticket, and followed him to see which compartment he took? Not Anna; what kind of thief stole from somebody and then bunked with them? He could hear something now in the corridor, voices as they neared.

Anna tossed her covers back. "Get in my bunk!" He was too astonished to protest, even when she reached over and killed the light and demanded, "Give me your blankets and pillow!"

"What?"

"You cannot travel without a passport and visa! Are you crazy or something?" She was acting as though he'd be thrown into prison, put up before a firing squad. He said, "I'll just explain—" but her panic was contagious. "Get down under my covers!" she said. "They will think I am the only one in the compartment. A messy sleeper, maybe, but alone." She snatched at his arm across the gap between them.

Later he would wonder why he obeyed her so unquestioningly; it must have been the disorientation of being woken, of the strange surroundings, of the lost passport. He burrowed down in her bunk. If it hadn't been so unbearably hot, it might have been intoxicating; he was tangled up in her bare legs, which were hard and muscled. She snarled at him, "Don't say a *word*," moments before someone rapped at the door of the compartment. He had a final moment of wondering if it might not be a better idea to come clean with the passport officials, surely they'd seen it before, but the door slid open, and then it was too late. He couldn't understand what anyone was saying, they were speaking either Romanian or Moldovan, but there were two of them, a man and a woman. Anna made her voice sound sleepy and reproachful, and he could tell she was saying *no, no, no* as they reached for the light switch. She must have convinced them, for they stepped into the lighted corridor to examine her documents. They all sounded awfully chummy, he thought. Maybe it was some kind of trick played by all three of them. Maybe it was an elaborate scheme to get him into some kind of trouble, plant drugs on him, make him disappear to some unknown cell block in the former Soviet Union. Maybe it was like that one movie he saw about the rich people who paid lots of money to torture tourists. Maybe they were terrorists. Maybe he was really, really paranoid.

Anna was laughing now and a twinge of jealousy surprised him—hadn't he made her laugh the same way just a few minutes ago? She hadn't thought he was funny at all. She was making fun of him. Briefly, dangerously, he thought he ought to jump out and surprise them all.

"Okay," she said. "Okay, they are gone." She flicked back the covers. "You can go now."

He said, daring, "I was hoping that was what passed for a courtship ritual in your country," but she didn't laugh again, and maybe the vocabulary was too difficult, but he felt himself flush as he settled himself back on his own bunk. She tossed over his blanket and pillow, and then reached into her own bag.

"Hungry?" she said. "Thirsty?" She passed him something wrapped in a napkin and a tall plastic water bottle. The thing in the napkin proved to be a bit of sweet crumbly cake.

"This isn't water," he said, and she laughed. "Of course it is not water," she said. "It's wine. My family made it. All Moldovans make wine." He took an experimental sip—he didn't know anything about wine, but it seemed okay. She laughed again. "In Moldova, we drink it like shots, like this," and she mimed doing it.

"But I don't have a shot glass," he said.

"Never mind," she said, still laughing. "*Noroc!* You have to say it. It means good luck. Drink some more, then give it here to me. You need some good luck."

He did as she said and passed it back. She took a swig as well and returned his "*Noroc!*" Now she was looking at him intently as he finished the slice of cake. "Do you have any money?" she said. "Or have you lost that too?"

He checked. This time at greater leisure, if indeed it could be called that, the frantic taking and shaking out of everything in his pack to discover that no, he had nothing, no passport, no money, no credit cards, not even his phone, which he'd dutifully used to photograph all of his important documents in case of just such an incident.

"We will need money to bribe the officials when we get off the train in Chişinău," she said. "I have some."

"A bribe, really?" he said. That sounded dangerous. And unnecessary. And dramatic.

"Of course," she said sharply.

If this was a scam that she was a part of, it had to be one of the weirdest ones ever. Maybe it was some kind of mail-order bride thing. David tried to figure out how that might work. He said, experimentally, "I'm engaged, you know. To someone back in America."

She was counting out her own notes, and she looked at him. "What has that got to do with anything?"

He was embarrassed, self-conscious, suddenly all too aware of his helplessness in a foreign place. "I don't know," he said. He thought about Claudia back at home, prickly and impatient, to whom he was sort of engaged. In a manner of speaking.

"Right," she said. "I will pay the officials. You can pay me back when you get back to America, whatever, okay? Once we are off this train, just follow me and don't talk and do what I say."

He said, "My cousin's meeting me at the station, actually. That's what I'm doing here. Visiting Natalie. She works here. With the Peace Corps."

"Good, then your cousin can fix things for you I am sure, but," Anna said darkly, "let me get you off the train first. Trust me on this."

Did he have any choice?

The sun was reluctantly burning its way through the clouds when they arrived at the station in Chişinău. In their tiny cabin prior to deboarding, Anna had dressed with skilled modesty and made herself up, transforming into something formidable in a miniskirt and spiked heels and (David thought) too much make-up. She ushered him past officials as she said she would, shoving small wads of cash into their hands and chattering away, and then they were safe and outside the train station, yet there was no Natalie.

"Perhaps you can phone your cousin," Anna suggested, and he'd had her number, but stored in the phone that was missing, along with everything else that mattered.

"I have her address!" he remembered, and he dropped his bag and went pawing through it again, and this time, thank goodness, finally something going right, he found the little memo book where he'd scribbled it down in case his phone battery died along with a folded-up map he'd printed off Google.

Anna took the memo book from him and looked at the address with an expression he couldn't read. When she lowered the paper, she said, "Is this some kind of joke?"

He didn't know what to say, so he didn't say anything.

Anna said, "This is *my* address. How did you get my address?"

This was too much. This was too far. This was definitely an elaborate scam, although he couldn't make head or tails of it.

He said, "You must think I'm an idiot," and he heard Claudia saying it to him as well. *Lost your passport? And your money? Went off with some woman . . . honestly, David, do you expect me to believe this?*

*I* don't really believe this, he thought. "It must be some kind of mistake," he said. "I must have written the address down wrong," although he knew he hadn't, knew he'd been painstaking because he'd been so worried about getting lost in a foreign country.

Anna looked both angry and hurt. Of course she was pretending, he told himself. "What is wrong with you?" she said. "I helped you when I didn't have to. Go on then. Go to your embassy or go try to find your cousin *at my flat*. I have had enough of your problems."

*The Vestige*

He watched her walk away, and she did, so decisively that he thought she was not bluffing and he must have been wrong. But that he would write down the wrong address and that it would be hers was a coincidence that simply beggared belief. She got into a taxi and was gone. Off to find an easier mark, he told himself.

He debated trying to find the embassy or consulate first, but he only had the paper map to Natalie's and anyway, he was exhausted and confused and desperately wanted a familiar face. He found himself wanting to talk to Claudia as well, but of course he had no way of phoning her and, anyway, she would have only been disapproving. *This call is costing too much money, David.* And: *you always screw up the details.* He just wouldn't mention any of it to her even though he had the feeling she'd get it out of him one way or another. It was something he'd admired about her even as it frightened him, her scathing intuition and dogged determination to get to the bottom of him. It was, he supposed, what love was all about—someone knowing you better than you knew yourself.

He estimated that the walk to Natalie's would take about two hours. That wasn't so far, really, and she would be able to help. She'd take him to the embassy and help him get to the bottom of it all. He wouldn't be the first traveller the embassy staff had seen who'd been robbed. And as soon as he got to Natalie's he could print out all the documents he'd sent to himself as well. David set off, then, glad for the sunny day and, despite the growling in his stomach and a passing wish for coffee, feeling hopeful. It had been a weird night. It would be a weird story to tell later (to everyone but Claudia). At least he still had most of his belongings. He hitched his pack on his shoulders and set off toward Natalie's apartment.

❦

The parts of Chişinău he walked through weren't much to look at. The train station itself had been colourful enough on the outside, but soon, he found himself walking through a section of the city that grew increasingly shabby. He wondered how long he had been walking, but the phone had been his only way of telling time.

He was looking forward to seeing Natalie again. They'd been close as children, and drifted apart as time and growing up got in the way. He spent his adolescence in his room playing video games. Natalie ran away from home three times. But she was the kind of rebel who always landed on her feet. She'd joined a punk band, married and divorced, finally got it together and gone to college where she'd studied education, then taught inner-city school kids before joining the Peace Corps and moving to Moldova. After he'd got engaged to Claudia, he'd found himself overcome with a desire to see Natalie again, even though they hadn't spoken in years and had lived such different lives. He'd gone to a community college, gotten a business degree, and worked as support staff in offices since graduating, still living in the same town he grew up in. A timid life, or at least it felt like one to him. When they'd been children, Natalie had always been his defender, the fierce one of the two of them. He knew instinctively that she and Claudia would not like one another. Maybe that was why he needed to see her one last time.

He'd never travelled outside of the United States before in his life, although at Claudia's insistence, they were planning a honeymoon at some resort in Mexico. The night train had been cheaper than a direct flight into Moldova, but, more importantly, it had also sounded exciting. The flight into Bucharest, the journey to the train station, and the process of purchasing the ticket and then boarding the train had all been new and almost impossibly adventurous. Now, he was frightened, and felt alone, and was sweating in his dress clothes—button-down shirt, nice trousers—he'd unwisely donned thinking you had to look respectable when you travelled. The sun was quite warm, and as he made his way past streets of concrete apartment buildings, he felt certain he would never be able to figure out which one was Natalie's. He cursed himself again for his carelessness. But why had Natalie not been there to meet him in the first place? She had promised.

The buildings had the grim look of American high-rise housing projects from the 'seventies. When he'd followed the map for as long as he could and still found himself unable to choose between them, he approached a group of young people with Natalie's address held out before him. They watched him warily, and he found himself gesticulating as though he were mute. He was embarrassed to speak English in front of them. Finally one of them, a blonde girl with a big grin who looked about fourteen, took him by the arm and led him away. She chattered away the entire time without seeming to mind that he clearly couldn't understand a word she was saying.

He was glad it was a girl and not the boys, because he'd have been wary of following them into the block she led him into. Inside, it was in even worse repair than he'd imagined. Graffiti scarred the walls, and the cold cement stairwell they climbed was unlit and crumbling and smelled of damp.

The girl moved just ahead of him, still chattering away, casting the occasional charming smile over her shoulder at him. He was a little concerned she'd misunderstood what he wanted, but she said "Natalie" a few times, so she must know her—or maybe he'd said Natalie's name first, before he lost the ability to speak at all? He couldn't remember.

At last they were out of the terrible stairwell and round a corner, and the girl skipped ahead of him and rapped hard on the first door on the left. When she did so it swung open of its own accord. For a moment he expected Anna to step out and berate him. Instinct pushed him across the threshold, a sense of emptiness before he confronted it. He took the place in quickly; it felt like a museum. Natalie had said she was renting an apartment from a family that had gone to the UK to work. He was surprised by the care and delicacy that had gone into its decoration: the touches of lace, the cabinet of what must surely be heirloom bric-a-brac, the heavy curtains that disguised the outside world and the fabrics and overstuffed furniture that gave the modest room a palatial feel. It was, or should have been, as cosy as the rest of the building was grim.

It should have been, and was not, because no one had been inside this apartment for a very long time. A gentle coating of dust lay across everything; the temperature, the atmosphere, the smell inside was the same as on the landing outside. He knew if he crossed to the stack of books on a small side table, they would be swollen with moisture and stuck together with mould.

David turned back to the girl. "I was looking for Natalie," he said, but the girl was gone.

He was suddenly exhausted: the heat, the hunger, the wine, the stress, all of it combined, and at the same moment he realised he had nowhere to go. He reeled over to the sofa. He tasted dust as he fell back onto its cushions, and fell into darkness.

David woke without opening his eyes and without confusion. He knew exactly where he was, on Natalie's couch in Natalie's apartment, and he thought he would lie there for a little bit longer with his eyes closed while he worked through the possibilities of what might have happened. One was that the woman who called herself Anna (for surely that was not her real name) had drugged him, and so his own perceptions could not be trusted. He could not think of any other possibilities, so he lay there a little bit longer with his eyes closed.

He suddenly missed Claudia so much he found her absence difficult to bear. He missed her calm, her dogged expectation of incompetence from everyone else that nevertheless ensured that things almost always ran smoothly, because she was prepared for every contingency. She was so capable. None of these things would have happened to him with Claudia along. He felt that a part of him might have been passing an unfair judgment on her earlier, mentally constructing a Claudia out of her worst qualities and none of her good ones. He opened his eyes.

Doing so proved to be anticlimactic, for there was only the ceiling overhead, and silence. He turned his head, and saw the apartment as it had been on his arrival: the lace, the bric-a-brac, the heavy furniture. He said, "Natalie?" experimentally, and there was no reply. Of course there was not. He admitted to himself for the first time that he was afraid. He said it out loud, trying it out. "I'm afraid." *Don't be silly, what are you afraid of, David?* That was Claudia's voice. I don't know, he told it. But that was a lie. I'm afraid to say the things I'm afraid of.

Just in case, he tried again. "Anna?" She had written him letters when they were kids that she signed that way. *I'm Anna when I get tired of being Natalie.* Of course there was no reply to that either.

He thought of Natalie as she'd looked in her most recent photos on Facebook. Last time he'd seen her, years ago, her honey-coloured hair had been dyed black and styled like Betty Page. But now she looked like the stereotypical California girl she was again, all healthy glow and wholesome toothy smile. He thought of her harder then, as though thinking of her could conjure her, her voice that was just a little lower than you'd expect, the way she smelled of roses and cigarettes and beer. She'd quit the last two, she'd told him, and the roses, well, she probably hadn't really smelled like roses. It was just the cheap body spray she'd worn as a teenager, but when he'd stood close enough to her to smell her it had enraptured him.

Natalie. Where was she in this city? Where was he, for that matter?

There was nothing else for it. He had to go to the embassy himself. He'd head back toward the centre of town and surely there had to be a tourist office, something, someone somewhere who spoke enough English to direct him there, and they would fix him up with a new passport and Claudia could wire him some money or whatever it was you did.

Or was it the consulate he needed? Were they even the same thing? His knowledge of such matters came from stitched-together pop culture references in action movies and spy thrillers. He hadn't really done any research prior to his trip because he'd expected Natalie to shepherd him around. If he wandered around asking people where the American embassy was, surely they could direct him. But then he imagined a foreigner coming to ask him how to get to their own embassy in a large American city. He'd have no idea.

He thought about wandering the streets, listening for an American accent that might indicate someone who could help him. The idea exhausted him. How many tourists even came here anyway? He was still very thirsty, so he got up and went over to the kitchen area and found a dusty glass in a cabinet. The water came out brown at first but then looked okay, and he rinsed the glass and drank some of the water. It tasted gritty and strange, but he supposed it wouldn't poison him. He found himself wondering if there was anything to eat in the apartment and began looking through more cabinets before remembering an apple he hadn't eaten on the flight. He found it in his bag, and sat on the edge of the sofa eating the rest of it. He half-expected it to have turned to maggots all in a tenor with this strangest of strange days, but in fact it was sweet and bright and crunchy, the only thing that seemed alive in this awful dead room.

He wondered then why it had occurred to him to think of the apartment as dead; then he got up again and walked around it, and into the second room that completed it, looking for some sign of Natalie. He opened a closet and saw some clothes hanging there that might be hers, but how would he know? He opened drawers, looking for something personal, looking for one of the letters he had written to her, but found nothing.

The young blonde girl had either played a trick on him or misunderstood who or what he was looking for. It was the only explanation. Nevertheless he did not want to leave; he found some sense of respite here in this gloomy and forgotten place, and he knew it would be gone again the moment he stepped back out into the street. He heaved the backpack onto his shoulders and trudged back down the stairs and outside, back toward the train station.

In the end he'd stopped people on the street until he found a couple who spoke English, and they had looked up the embassy on their phones and mapped its location for him. After that, everything had seemed easy, because he'd imagined he would get to the embassy and would be unable to prove that he existed, would in fact not exist, would find his email account gone and a collect call to Claudia rejected because he'd stepped into a parallel world where he did not exist in Claudia's life. There had been some hassle—he'd had to make a police report, for one, no small task—but both they and the embassy staff had dealt with foreigners with emergencies before and his was relatively easy to solve, with all of his documents saved in his email and a girlfriend who could wire him the money he needed. Claudia herself wasn't angry at all when he reached her by phone, only concerned. By the close of day he had cash in hand, a temporary passport on the way and a story to tell, although he wasn't sure who he could tell it to.

In some ways, he found himself disappointed that it had all been as easy as it was. Natalie's absence would make more sense if he were missing from the world as well.

But there would be a logical explanation; there had to be. Mixed-up dates, mixed-up addresses, all the mix-ups in the world had converged at once and when he contacted Natalie the following day it would all make sense again. No more mix-ups.

Instead, he spent the next few nights in a youth hostel. He found an internet café, and looked up Natalie's address and phone number again in his email. The address matched the one he had on paper, and all their messages back and forth still existed, sitting on a server somewhere and appearing one after another on his screen as he clicked to open them. The phone number appeared to be out of service. He wrote her an email and sent it off without hope. He went to the train station the next morning and waited for the arrival of the night train from Bucharest and he watched people deboard, expecting Anna to be among them, or Natalie to be wandering about, waiting for him on the wrong day, but he saw neither of them.

He hailed a taxi outside the station and handed Natalie's address to the driver. He had the sense that if he tried it again, on a different day, he could get it right. The driver took him back to a familiar set of buildings. David tapped on the address and held out cash to the driver, pointing to the building and hoping he was indicating he wanted the driver's help in finding the place. The driver took him back up the stairs to the same apartment. David tried to pay him extra and the driver refused, seeming anxious to be away.

He went back again, three times in total. The door was never locked, and each time he waited and listened in the solitude for someone who never came.

Each time he dozed off. The third time, he woke and found a slice of cake wrapped in paper and a water bottle full of wine sitting in the middle of the dining room table and a sense of someone having just left. No—someone was still in the apartment. He bolted upright and raced into the other room. Again the sense of a presence. Someone was here and not here. He could almost smell the person, almost hear the person, in a silence that he could almost but not quite put a name to.

He ate the cake and drank some of the wine, and left the rest of it. He knew as he did so that he would not return again. He said, "*Noroc!*" when he drank the wine as Anna had told him to.

In the evenings he went out for shish kebabs or Turkish pizza, both of which seemed to be popular menu items in Chişinău restaurants. He ate and he drank wine and listened to the chatter around him, which he could not understand. There was a great comfort in it, like being invisible.

On the last day, he stopped by the Peace Corps office to ask after Natalie. It was anticlimactic, as he'd known it would be, and that was why he had not bothered to do so earlier. It was more a matter of tying off a loose end than expecting any progress. They had not heard of her, or said they had not. And what reason would they have to lie about it?

He shared a compartment with a boisterous family on the

train back to Bucharest where his flight was delayed. He sat in a bar at the airport and had three quick shots of whiskey, one after another, until a woman came and sat two stools down from him. He felt her looking at him and shifted his body in the opposite direction so he could not see her. He could smell her: like roses. He left his fourth shot untouched, and glancing her way when he left, he caught an impression of wide eyes with an interesting scar above an unplucked brow.

He waited in the departure lounge looking out at the night sky. That was something he and Natalie had enjoyed doing when they had been kids. Imagine, they would say to one another. Imagine, we sent people up there once. Imagine if aliens came down from there. What would they do or say? Maybe we were the aliens, he'd said. Maybe we came here from another planet. Natalie would say, that's silly. Haven't you ever heard of the fossil record? Everything and everybody leaves traces behind. Nothing just disappears.

Of course here at the airport there was too much light pollution, and the stars themselves might have gone out for all he could see of them. They left no traces of themselves at all, and still appeared to be missing as his plane lifted off and sheared the oblivious sky.

# The Unknown Chambers

*I*n the lightless places he waits, in the dark that is darker
than the dark of the day and the dark of the night and
the dark of the soul, he waits he waits for his father he
says 'father I am waiting for you' and the sun is falling in a
blistered sky and the night is roaring in and still he waits.

– *Asmodeus* (1936)
Garland William Stevens

*Stevens produced a single novel, the short, bizarre*
Asmodeus, *which has drawn comparisons to the better-
known* The Night Land *by William Hope Hodgson.
In addition to his other writing, Stevens published at
least thirty stories in* Weird Tales, Unknown, Strange
Tales of Mystery and Terror, Small Hours, *and several
other magazines between 1923-1940. Most of his
stories remain uncollected, but in 2013, Catherine J.
Framer edited a small press volume that was published
by Gloaming Press,* Lost Worlds: The Weird Tales of
Garland William Stevens. *It contained a dozen stories
including his two best-known, "A Tale of a Hollow Earth"
(*Weird Tales, *1934) and "In the Quarters of the Lost"
(*Unknown, *1939). Framer was at the time a graduate
student working on a dissertation about Stevens.*

– *The Dictionary of Weird Horror* (2019)

"Is Asmodeus seeking this?"

Catherine jumped. "What?"

"I asked if anyone was reading this."

Reality righted itself. A stoop-shouldered man of indeterminate age with a craggy face and a wad of tobacco in his cheek was pointing at the newspaper on the edge of the plastic orange table where she sat. "No," she said, "no, go ahead and take it." The spell was broken. Outside the window was not the weird world of Garland William Stevens's ruined plantations and degenerate Southern families but a drab four-lane highway and a gas station across the street. Around her, the Bojangles fast food restaurant was rapidly filling up with the post-church crowd: hefty middle-aged ladies and their balding husbands, small children in Sunday finery, grandmas and great-grandmas with walkers, and shiny-faced teenagers. What Garland William Stevens would have called the filthy mess of humanity. Small wonder really that the town of Eudora did nothing to honour the man, given the contempt with which he had chronicled its perceived shortcomings. In fact, most likely no one around her had ever even heard of him.

Catherine gobbled down the rest of her ham and cheese biscuit, shoved her tablet into her bag, and headed back out to her car. Back on the road, she soon turned off the four-lane onto a poorly maintained two-lane, bumping over railway tracks. She passed two abandoned granite sheds, long metal buildings, the stonecutting shops where local families had made their fortune carving monuments—tombstones, that is—out of the granite unearthed from quarries throughout the county until China proved able to do it more cheaply and the industry died, leaving the town with nothing. She supposed that at one time the four-lane must have brought visitors to Eudora as well, back in the day when people used to travel by state highways instead of national interstate. Now it was just another tiny Southern town closing in on itself and clinging to its outmoded ways as a confusing and frightening twenty-first century unfolded before it.

But commerce was not her concern, and she drove on as the road grew rough with potholes and narrowed even more, and then pavement gave way to Georgia red clay. She slowed, as the recent heavy summer rains had turned the clay to mud, and more than once her car skidded gently toward the wide ditches on either side. She wondered what she would do if she met another vehicle on the narrow lane, but then she rounded a corner and there it was. The old Stevens homeplace.

Catherine left her car on what must have once been a grand circular drive outside and approached the place. It was in less disrepair than she expected given that the man had no heirs and the place seemed to be owned by an out-of-state company that she had been unable to get a response from. The house was more modest than she had imagined as well. Stevens had loathed the place, of course, like he loathed everything. Despising his slave-owning forefathers as evidence of the essential evil that poisoned humanity, he was equally contemptuous toward abolitionists and their civil-rights activist descendants—"do-gooders", he called them— finding their efforts exercises in futility against a backdrop of cruelty and indifference. In Stevens's worldview, savagery toward one another was the natural state of humanity; any efforts on the part of the species to rehabilitate itself were at best pointless and at worst roads to hell paved with good intentions.

Or *was* this his belief system? That the man had been virtually hypergraphic was both a blessing and a curse for an ambitious young graduate student. During his short life he had not only produced a not-insubstantial volume of published fiction and nonfiction but reams of letters, notes, and diaries. So difficult and contentious a figure was Stevens that he was little-studied and thus largely unknown, and much of his archive remained unsorted decades after his death. As repulsed as the man was by people, he carried on a prodigious correspondence with dozens of them, and from the one side of the exchange she was able to read, those correspondents praised his unfailing generosity and sensible advice. It was as though having established for himself that humanity as a whole was a disgusting, bestial evolutionary dead-end, he set out to contradict this assessment with his own behaviour at every turn. These paradoxes, the fact that she didn't yet really know what shape her dissertation would take, were part of what made the research so intriguing.

"They're waiting at the edge."

She jumped, and whirled round. The speaker looked to be in his twenties, lanky and blond, wearing a black t-shirt, jeans, and a trucker hat. He was also startlingly homely, with features overlarge in an otherwise too-small face. She snapped, "What did you say?"

"I said, are you the lady from the college? They sent me your letter. The owners. They said you would be coming by."

She frowned. "Nobody ever replied to me."

The man shrugged. "They wouldn't. They don't never answer nobody about nothing." She couldn't place his accent; it was thick, Southern but not local.

She said, "Who are you?"

"I'm the caretaker." The man extended his hand and pulled back his lips in what she assumed must be a smile; she wished he hadn't. There seemed to be too many teeth in his mouth. She felt off-kilter; she had not expected anyone to be here, and here he was, and he knew who she was and why she was here and so far she still didn't know anything about him.

She was being silly. This was a terrific opportunity, particularly since she'd never imagined she might be able to go inside.

"But I'm afraid I can't help you with your research," he said. "I don't know nothing about this guy. My family's not from around here. I just look after the place."

"I promise, just being shown around the place is a huge help," she said. "Where are you from?"

"Down south Georgia. My people come from the swamp," he said, in a way that let her know no further questioning would be welcome. Well, she didn't care who he was or where he came from anyway. If he didn't want to small talk, all the better; she could get on with the business of exploring the house.

"We can go inside, can't we?" she said, but he already had keys in his hands and she followed him up onto the wide front porch.

When the door swung open, she took a step back in surprise. Whatever she had expected, it was not this. Based on the interior of the house, anyone would be forgiven for thinking that Stevens had not only not been dead for decades but had only stepped out to run an errand that morning and would be back if she just waited around long enough. The place was minimally furnished but beyond that it *felt* lived in.

But of course. "*You* live here?" she said to the caretaker. He shrugged. "I'm sorry," she said. "I didn't know anyone was out here. I couldn't get any information from anyone about the place and I just assumed it was abandoned. I didn't mean to disturb you." She almost added *I can come back at a better time if you want* but bit back the words before they were out. There would never be a better time: she might never have another chance like this.

"It's left the same as when *he* lived here," the caretaker said.

"Oh. So you live here, or . . . " She left the question dangling so he could pick it up and answer it, but he remained silent. "Oh, God," she said. "Sorry for my rudeness." She held out her hand. "I'm Catherine, and what was your name?"

"Don't matter none. I'm just the caretaker."

"That's fine, but it would really help if I could get your name. For my research."

"Let me show you the downstairs first," he said, heading off any further questions. She followed him round the spartan rooms. What seemed to be the living room contained only a single wooden chair and a small, rickety table that appeared to function as a desk, stacked high as it was with papers and open books. The caretaker hustled her through too quickly to get a closer look at them. The remainder of the tour was equally rushed; a kitchen with old but modern appliances, an upstairs bedroom that was as bare as the living room save for a single bed and another wooden chair, and a whole host of rooms with closed doors that she was not invited to look behind.

She tried one last question. "Just to be clear . . . those books and papers in the living room are yours, right? They aren't unarchived papers from Mr. Stevens, are they?"

"That's all I can show you of the place," the man said. "I hope it helped you out. You ought not to come back here."

"I'm sorry for being so nosy," she said. "It's just, you know, there's been almost no work done on Mr. Stevens, and so primary sources are mostly all I have to go on. Which is kind of simultaneously a scholar's dream and nightmare. Would it be possible for me to contact you again at some point?"

"I got to get to work now. We ain't set up for tourists here, you know."

The protest that she was not a tourist—and what tourist could possibly be interested in this anyway—died on her lips. "I'm sorry I disturbed you," she said. Driving back into town and heading toward home, something niggled at the back of her mind, something she felt she had missed, but she could not put her finger on what it was.

*Degeneracy is the disease of the human race. For every lie told by Biblical sources there are truths as well, and none so true as that tale of the Fall of Man. From the time man drew his first breath, this disease seized him, and whatever gifts might have been innate were quickly subsumed by his lust: for power, for violence, for sex. The Garden of Eden withered and died with the exhale of that first breath. Human beings tell tales about monsters to hide their own monstrosity.*

– Unpublished Papers (c. 1925)

"The natural explanation is that Garland William Stevens himself is still alive, having achieved some sort of unnatural longevity just like a character in one of his stories." The bar where Catherine and her best friend Marisol had met for drinks was starting to fill up with students even though it was a Sunday night, and she had to shout it in order to be heard. Three beers in, her theory did not seem so unlikely.

"Or," Marisol said, "the so-called caretaker is his progeny, the result of some kind of weird mixing with an ancient inhuman race of beings." Marisol had sensibly dropped out of their PhD program, abandoning her own dissertation on women in cannibal films two years earlier to start a catering business, a shift in focus that spawned its share of jokes both in and out of the department. She still worked the same insane hours she had as a graduate student but she actually got paid well for doing so and still had time to read for pleasure, unlike Catherine. And she'd devoted some of that spare time to remaining Catherine's first reader, even before her adviser, helping her start to shape years' worth of writing and notes into something resembling a critical analysis and a book-length dissertation.

"Both, probably," Catherine said. "Why couldn't I have picked someone normal and easy to study like . . . well, pretty much anyone else?"

"Because your parents never told you, but you were actually adopted, and are also the unnatural progeny of Garland William Stevens, drawn back to your birthplace and destiny by some inexorable force . . . "

"Oh god. All of these scenarios just write themselves, don't they? I've been mired in reading this stuff for so long I've pretty much lost touch with reality, but what's your excuse?"

"Listening to you for the last few years."

"I'm not that single-minded, am I?" She saw her friend's face. "I am, aren't I? Jesus. Sorry. But seriously, everything about it was weird, and there was more weird stuff about it I can't put my finger on too."

Marisol was looking at her more seriously now. "Like, he was a creep or something? You probably shouldn't have gone out there on your own."

"No, not weird like that. Anyway, who would've ever imagined someone would be out there in the first place? No, it was like something I saw that didn't register consciously. Or something I heard, or smelled, or even just a feeling."

Marisol grinned. "I have the feeling you need more beer."

"I have the feeling I have to be on campus before eight tomorrow morning to proctor an exam so, no, I'm gonna take a rain check on that one. But more seriously, can you do me a favour?"

"Depends on what it is." They had been friends for more than a decade; it was how they always answered the question, and neither had ever refused the other.

"If you're not working tomorrow afternoon, I want to drive back out there. It's going to piss off Mr. Caretaker, but if he's that mad about it, he can just accuse me of trespassing and tell me to leave and I will."

Marisol frowned. "Are you sure? What if he's one of those shoot first ask questions later assholes?"

Catherine shook her head. "No, if there's one thing we don't have to worry about, it's that. He's not the type."

"How can you *know*?"

"Look, I'm not asking you to go back out there with me because I'm scared to go by myself. I'm asking you because I need a second set of eyes and ears and another brain to give me your impressions. There's something weird and very much *not dangerous* going on out there, and you know how I've been spinning my wheels on this dissertation lately. Please, Marisol. You *know* what an impossible dream it is to get a tenure-track job in the humanities these days. If I could come up with something truly ground-breaking and something that had both academic *and* popular appeal I'd be—well, I wouldn't be set, but it would help me out a lot, and it could be life changing for me. And if there's more stuff out there, or if this caretaker guy could give me information . . . "

Marisol said, "How could you need more information? Especially from some random who just lives out there? Or even use it? You've still got mountains of material in the archives you haven't gotten to yet." But Catherine could see it in her face as her resolve wavered, and she almost felt bad about giving her the hard sell—almost.

"Remember the time you took off on a road trip with that French guy you'd just met and then called me at two in the morning from Mobile, Alabama and said he'd taken off in the middle of the night and stuck you with the motel bill and anyway he wasn't French? And I drove all night to come and get you?"

"All right," Marisol said. "I'll go, but if we end up abducted as part of a master plan to breed their nightmare progeny, I'm totally blaming you."

Catherine grinned. "Deal. And this time tomorrow we'll be back here talking about what a weird freaking place that town is."

"Okay." Marisol pushed herself up from the bar stool. "I'm off tomorrow, and I'm not going home yet. There are too many cute boys in here to go home. Like that one over there. I'll see you tomorrow."

"I'll just be headed back to my nun cell," Catherine said, but Marisol was already striding across the bar.

Catherine liked knowing what awaited her at home: stacks of books and papers, what the writer Fritz Leiber had called the scholar's mistress. She lay down at night with Garland William Stevens and woke beside him in the morning, but the metaphor failed there; she thought of her subject not as a lover but a mentor, a guide even. Sometimes even, she thought, *psychopomp*, but those were only in the darkest times, and she did not tell anyone about those.

*As the human race embraces degeneracy, it also fears and despises it. This is not the degeneracy of everyday standards of behaviour and morality the small minded among us fret over, for man is in truth without morality beyond an ever-changing social construct. This is a terror of literal physical and mental degeneracy of the species, and it explains our repulsion toward invertebrate forms of life, toward the types of creatures scientists find existing*

*on the bottom of the ocean, toward snakes and insects
and all the other beings that remind us what we were
before we were human and what we will be again when
our nature asserts itself over our intelligence and draws
us back into darkness.*

– Unpublished Papers (n.d.)

The following morning, Catherine headed over to the rare
books room once she'd discharged her duties supervising
freshman exams. She reflected, as she let herself in, on what
a sheer stroke of luck her course of study had been—whether
good or bad luck remained to be seen. She'd arrived at the
University of Georgia primed to study advertising and make
her fortune cynically hawking products to those too well off
to care that they were being lied to. Her friends gave her
shit about taking her writing and design skills and selling
out, but she didn't care; she'd been raised in near-poverty,
with parents who'd always had a scheme that was going to
turn things around for the family and never did. She'd grown
up in clothes from the Salvation Army, nourished on crappy
fast food and cheap supermarket staples, and steeped in the
knowledge that one inconvenient illness or untimely car
breakdown could mean an eviction. She was determined to
lead a different life.

So it was sheer luck that had landed her a work-study
position in the rare books room of the library, and luck that
within her first weeks there she'd stumbled across the archives
of an obscure Southern writer known as Garland William
Stevens. She'd never heard of him, and neither had anyone
else she spoke to; apparently even in his lifetime he had
been little-known, composing stories and books that veered

from grim little horror vignettes to a bizarre experimental novel to a book-length philosophical musing on the ultimate meaningless of life and the degradation of being trapped in a human skin. The last of his line, his short and unhappy life had ended in 1940 when he was thirty-five years of age. The possible causes of his death ranged from tetanus to tick fever to tuberculosis (various claims he made in the final delirious lines he penned) to an ill-advised effort to kick his alcoholism cold turkey (her theory, particularly given the delusions and hallucinations he appeared to have suffered in the final weeks of his life).

What she had pieced together about his life story had been bizarre and grim. Both of his parents had been born during the Civil War. Stevens's family had been among the most prominent in Eudora but appeared to have lost their wealth well before the war for reasons that were unclear. Both parents grew up nursing a sense of bitter entitlement and loss. Garland had been born when they were both in their forties, having long since abandoned the idea of having any children. His father had been a virulent racist, penning regular send-them-back-to-Africa op-eds for the local paper and articles about the inherent superiority of the white race— and the town indeed had a reputation for being particularly inhospitable to non-whites even by the standards of the time and place. Garland had despised both of his parents, his father in particular, but lived with and cared for them his entire life until their deaths. In the final decade of both their lives, they suffered multiple strokes and dementia, and the already isolated, angry man fell deeper into an abyss. All of them had died the same year, several months apart, first the father, then the mother, then Garland himself.

The university had no record of who was responsible for the donation of Stevens's archives decades earlier or who had originally accepted them, and no one really knew who was responsible for them or what was to be done with them because in a library there is always more to be done than there is time to do it. And so they had mostly sat there, largely undisturbed, until she had come across them. And began reading. And reading and reading. And before she knew it, she had changed her major to literature and set off on the very path of hard work and penury she had sworn to avoid, struggling through graduate school and unsure whether she was onto something ground breaking and revolutionary that would make her a scholarly superstar or something obscure and irrelevant that was gradually turning her into a crank. She told herself the first; she suspected the second.

Over the past decade, since her first discovery of the archives, she had done a great deal to organise them and even made efforts to bring Stevens to wider attention. She genuinely did believe that at his best he was truly a talented stylist, easily on the same level as any of the other great regional writers like Faulkner and O'Connor. She had managed to interest a couple of small presses enough to allow her to edit one book of short fiction and a reprint of one of his "philosophical musings" as he dubbed his nonfiction work, but even the obsessive-minded customers of specialty presses had shown little interest in her discovery. Around her, friends finished their schooling and began real careers and had disposable incomes and partners and spouses and some were even starting on homes and children while she felt herself growing smaller and dustier and more desperate deep in the bowels of the same rare book collection where she'd been hiding out since the first quarter of her freshman year of college. She constantly questioned herself, but she could not deny that in the end she still believed it was worthwhile. For one, it wasn't just the scholarly pleasure of discovering an unknown writer—she actually *appreciated* the work of Garland William Stevens, thought it the work of a twisted, misanthropic genius, rife with metaphor about the ugliest side of the human condition. And for another, she knew she was ever on the verge of a great discovery. She could not say why; she had no evidence to show what had led her to this conclusion. Instead, it was a growing certainty that rose from the deep waters of intuition. She knew that it was not wishful thinking. She knew that her work on Garland William Stevens was the most important thing she could possibly do with her life.

*They gathered in their churches day and night, worshipping every hour of every day, churches that might have been churches of the damned had they souls to damn or a god to damn them, but by then they understood what must one day be understood by all: that there is nothing, nothing but the depths, the deep ones, and an unfortunate evolutionary error that calls itself the inheritor of the earth for the few milliseconds that it believed in its own dominion, not just of the planet, but throughout the universe.*

— *Asmodeus* (1936)

Eudora was about an hour's drive and a world away. As they entered the city limits the following day, Marisol commented, "They sure do love Jesus here, don't they?"

"Was it the multiple signs about repenting, or the dozen churches you see just after crossing the county line?"

"It's kind of disturbing. I mean, it's not the usual sort of bland Bible-belty stuff. The signs were creepy, like 'Children of the Corn' stuff or something."

"Luckily we're not in the Midwest. No need to worry about demon kids coming out of a cornfield after us."

"Oh, pull over," Marisol said. "This might be Creepytown but they also have a Bojangles. I want a biscuit. I had a late night."

"So many cute boys, so little time?"

"Something like that."

Back inside the same fast food restaurant, Catherine said, "Do you notice anything odd?"

Marisol looked around. "Well, everyone looks a tad overdressed. I mean, I realise there's not a lot to do around here but surely a trip to Bojangles doesn't require suiting up in your Sunday best."

"They all looked like this yesterday too, only I didn't think it was a big deal because, well, it was Sunday. I thought they were all coming from church."

As she spoke, one man detached himself from the line in front of them and went over to a small man in an ill-fitting suit alone at a table and bellowed, "Great sermon today, reverend! Praise the Lord! What are you doing sitting over here all by your lonesome?"

"Oh. Well, then, I guess they go to church all the time here," Marisol murmured. "Definitely 'Children of the Corn'. We'll turn around and leave now if we know what's good for us."

"Probably they really don't have anything better to do than go to church. Nobody has jobs any more since the granite industry died."

"They look—kind of messed up?" Marisol observed, and Catherine saw what she had missed the previous day. All around them most people had unhealthy complexions shading to a kind of waxy greyness Catherine identified with her grandfather's face in the final days of his life. They moved oddly as well, and she had the thought that it was as though they weren't accustomed to using their limbs in quite this manner or were concealing deformities under their clothes. But then she came from a small town, too, not terribly unlike Eudora, and everyone there seemed to be everyone's cousin. Catherine herself had a sprawling batch of relatives back home. Maybe in Eudora they were all just a little bit too closely related to one another.

"Also," and now Marisol was whispering, "um, what did they do with all the Black people here? Or Mexicans? I'm feeling a little unwelcome truth be told."

"It's not a historically tolerant community," Catherine whispered back.

"Fuck that," Marisol said, "I'm getting my biscuit to go. You didn't tell me it was some kind of KKK enclave."

"It's not really that. It's—they don't like any outsiders. The town's always been that way, if you go back and look at census records. Nobody really moves here, It's just the same families have been here since the nineteenth century."

"I can't imagine why, it has so much to offer. I'm already thinking of relocating myself."

Back in the car, Catherine commented, "I know this town's been in dire economic straits over the last ten years or so, but I didn't think it meant they just spent all their time in church."

"It was probably a big funeral or something," Marisol said.

"Yeah, you're probably right." Catherine started the car but felt unconvinced. "It didn't seem like a funeral," she said after a few minutes.

"Look, you're the one who insisted on bringing me out here on the grounds that there was nothing creepy to worry about. You can't go making things creepy now."

"Garland William Stevens *is* creepy. There's no getting around that."

"I can't argue with that," Marisol said. "Also, this biscuit is gross. What the fuck do they put in it?" She dropped it back into its bag and tossed the entire thing out the window.

"Marisol!"

"Sorry. You can make a citizen's arrest on me for littering if you want but it smelled awful too. I was going to puke if I kept it in the car with us. So, what's with all the old granite sheds? You were saying . . . "

"Just that it was the industry here, and now it's mostly closed down. Now there's abandoned granite sheds and quarries all over the county. Actually, do you mind if we make a stop before we head out there?" Catherine didn't wait to hear an answer; she was already doing a U-turn on the four-lane.

"Got a sudden hankering to go to church yourself now?" Marisol said.

"The local museum," Catherine said. She drove a few blocks, turned off the main road, and parked in front of a nondescript two-story granite building with a huge glass front. "Let's go in," she said.

"Are you going to tell me what's up?"

"Not until I'm sure." Inside, she thrust a few dollars for their admissions at the bland-faced man working the front desk. The man said to her, "He waits, changed."

"What?"

"The rates changed." The man tapped the sign beside the register. Catherine sighed and gave him two more dollars.

She had been here so many times that she knew exactly what she was looking for, and went to the enormous stone figure of a man in the middle of the place. It was lying on its side, legless and broken at the torso, about twenty feet long and several feet across, surrounded by a set of worn velvet ropes.

"What *is* this thing?" Marisol asked. "It's hideous."

"This," said Catherine, "was meant to be a statue commemorating the Civil War, from around the turn of the last century; 1905, to be exact. He's supposed to be a Confederate soldier, only the statue was carved by an Italian artist, and he—well, let's just say he wasn't quite in tune with what people wanted. The thing was torn down by angry townspeople on the day of its dedication, and nobody cared enough to right it—eventually, it was buried. They just unearthed it about ten years ago, when they opened the museum."

"Fascinating," Marisol said, in a tone that said she found it exactly the opposite. "And you just have to come back and visit it from time to time?"

Catherine said, "It's the face on the statue. I had to be sure."

"Sure about what?"

She took a deep breath, because she knew how she was going to sound. Marisol was going to say that the research had finally gotten to her, that she was going to start imagining things just as Garland William Stevens had done in the final weeks of his life.

She said, "The statue. Its face. It's the caretaker."

*The horrors birthed themselves from the quarries. Those who first dug deep into the earth and stone found them sleeping there and woke them, and were driven mad by their hideousness, and then mated with them, and if they did not then die from the shame, brought others back with them. These orgiastic frenzies of worship and lust and annihilation might go on for days or even weeks. It was said by some that their cities were so vast and so unspeakable that they broke the human mind . . .*

– "A Tale of a Hollow Earth" (1934)

❦

Back in the car, Marisol was still laughing and shaking her head. Of all the reactions Catherine expected—shock, horror, concern—this was not one of them. "You *have* been working too hard," she said. "I bet when you shut your eyes at night all you see is Stevens's manuscripts, and now you're seeing hundred year old statues in living men's faces. Maybe what you need *is* a live dude for a night or two . . . "

"I'm serious," Catherine said for the third time. "Look, you'll see when we get out there."

"I'm sorry," Marisol said. "I'm not making fun of you, I swear. It just sounds crazy. You know what? I bet this dude totally looks like that statue back there. I don't even know why it cracked me up so much, it just did. You know how those things happen. It's like when I was a kid, we noticed my brother looked just like the boy on that one commercial— hey, are you okay to drive?"

Catherine's hands were shaking. She lay them flat on the steering wheel to still them. "I'm okay," she said. "I'm just a little freaked out. You know, I've been here so many times. I've got sketches of that thing—Stevens was intrigued with stories of it even though he never saw it himself because it was destroyed the same year of his birth, and they didn't find it till decades after he was dead. That was the thing that was in the back of my mind yesterday, the thing that was bothering me. The caretaker's—his resemblance. That's all."

"Yep," Marisol said. "Look, I seriously doubt the caretaker is a golem. Or a homunculus. Or whatever it is he would be. I think we can clear that up right here and now."

"You know what," Catherine said suddenly, "I don't think it's such a good idea after all, us going out there. You were right."

She could feel Marisol's incredulous gaze on her without even turning her head.

"I was *what*? When have you *ever* admitted somebody else was right? Look, I know what this is about."

"I do so say people are right sometimes. Don't I?"

Marisol said, "You've just now decided that there's something dangerous out there and like a heroine in a poorly constructed horror movie *that we would yell our damn heads off at all the way through* you're going to go out there on your own and investigate it."

Catherine sat for a moment before she replied. "Okay, fine. Is there anything you can't figure out about me?"

"Why you want to devote yourself to Garland William Stevens."

"Anyway," Catherine said. "You'll see what I mean about the statue when you meet the caretaker."

*We have come to the end of everything that is or ever shall be.*

– "In the Quarters of the Lost" (1939)

She would not have been surprised if, on her return, the house had fallen into disrepair, its state of the previous day the result of some glamour, but it was as sturdy and well-kept as she remembered. Marisol sat beside her, gripping her phone like an emergency was imminent.

"What are we going to do?"

"I just want to talk to him again."

"Didn't he tell you to leave and not come back?"

"Well, but I won't take up that much of his time. And I just want you to tell me what you think about him."

Catherine got out of the car. She had to press on because she knew Marisol was right. She shouldn't have come back here at all. She turned around to tell Marisol that if something happened, If she disappeared, if anything, she should just drive away, she shouldn't feel bad, she shouldn't think about it at all, but that sounded crazy. And that would only panic Marisol and she would make them leave.

Catherine went up on the porch and peered in all the windows, but she couldn't see what was inside. There was no sign of the caretaker. She had always been able to explain anything to Marisol except this, the compulsion she had toward Stevens and his work. Marisol said she was just driven, and that it was a good thing, an admirable thing, but it was a drive that scared her. Because it was a drive without any sense to it. Who really did care about Garland William Stevens besides her? The world didn't need Stevens and his bottomless nihilistic despair. She was unsure what she found more appalling, the knowledge that her years of painstaking study would probably in the end leave her qualified for little more than a minimum-wage service job, or the sheer scope of Stevens's loathsome worldview, expanding as it did to encompass every living being save for the savage, primordial beasts at the heart of his fiction. As much as she tried to assume a disinterested scholarly attitude toward his work, in fact she found herself alternately repelled and consumed by the man's madness.

Almost without thinking, she tried the door, and the doorknob turned in her hand.

She pushed it open, and called out, "Hello? Is anyone there? It's Catherine Framer, from the university. I just wanted to ask you a few more questions."

In the silence that followed, she turned back and gave a thumbs-up sign in Marisol's direction accompanied by a big smile she did not feel. Marisol looked so worried and vulnerable sitting in the passenger seat, and she felt a rush of emotions toward her—affection, concern, but most of all a sorrow so profound that she gasped as it flooded her even as she was unable to make any sense of it. Then the sorrow passed and left her feeling empty, hollowed-out, and then there was a small space where she knew she would turn back after all, and then she did not.

*I returned last night to that place, to their place, to that monstrous city on the edge of the world in the bowels of the earth. The city has teeth; the city shrieks, but not at me, because it no more notices me than I notice microscopic beings on my own flesh. Time and space turn inside out there, and reason ceases to be. I stood for a moment and for a thousand years on the edge of what I could only think of as hell. My flesh cracked and my bones turned to powder and the city devoured itself and spat itself back up again. It was planet-sized; no, larger; it was an entire galaxy, its own universe: suns, worlds flared and died within its immense gates.*

– Unpublished Papers (1940)

"Hello," she said again, but only from habit, because she was certain she would not be answered. The interior of the house was just as she had seen it the previous day, but now she could explore at her leisure. She went over to the desk with the stacks of books and papers and pawed through them. The books all appeared to be very old, and none of them were in English; several did not use an alphabet she recognised. Two were handwritten, one in something similar to but not quite Arabic script. She could not read most of the papers either, which were not old and definitely not part of the Stevens archive. Some of them were covered not in words at all but in symbols and drawings of ancient creatures with no eyes or limbs, with notations such as "cephalopod, Paleozoic era". There were tracings of fossils with latitudinal and longitudinal locations scribbled next to them and notations regarding dates of discovery.

She took out her phone and began photographing the papers, but she quickly found them so distressing that she shoved them all aside. They overwhelmed her with that same revulsion that Stevens had written about, and perhaps he was right. Perhaps such sights wakened an instinctive, atavistic terror: one of the few things that could remind humans what late arrivals they were to this earth, and how fragile was their tenure.

How his parents must have resented what they imagined to be the decay of their own society around them; how they must have loathed the sense that their way of life was passing into irrelevance. As different as they were, both father and son attempted to stem the despairing realisation of their own insignificance with fortresses of words. Not for the first time, Catherine wondered about the parents' deaths; two mad, helpless old people trapped in this house and their failing bodies with an increasingly demented son. It wouldn't have taken much, just a palm placed over a sleeping nose and mouth. First one, then the other. Afterwards the guilt would have driven him to an alcoholic despair followed by a final, fatal bid to sober up, at which point his lifelong imaginings seemed to him to become reality: in those final weeks, his writings had become frenzied, surreal, barely coherent descriptions of a nightmare subterranean dwelling beneath the house that opened onto another, horrific dimension where the creatures from his stories tormented him without mercy.

She heard a noise then from upstairs, that of someone treading on floorboards, and a thump and a sound like something heavy being dragged, and it brought her to her senses. What had she been thinking, letting herself into someone's house, poking through their private papers? She scrambled for the front door, suddenly in a panic, and raced across the porch and threw herself into the driver's seat.

"What the hell happened in there?" Marisol said.

"Nothing," Catherine said, "nothing happened. There's nothing in there." She tried to catch her breath, which was too fast and too shallow. She shut her eyes and saw all the closed doors inside the house that she had not been allowed to open, and she wondered what lay behind them. "You know," she said, "all this was ocean once. First it was ocean and then it was swamp and everywhere creatures like things you'd see in nightmares, only worse. And someday it's going to be ocean again. Maybe even in our lifetimes if they don't fix the climate—what do you think?"

Marisol said, "I want to go home."

Catherine started the car and forced herself to guide it deliberately back onto the road, and they didn't speak at all on the journey back into town. Passing through Eudora, Catherine noticed just how shabby and depleted the town truly was: deserted shopping centres with weeds sprouting through the asphalt, shuttered gas stations, and a main road that was almost empty of other vehicles. She stopped at a red light and wondered why it was there, because surely there was never enough traffic to require it. The only signs of life were at the museum, the churches, and the single fast food restaurant. How was it possible for a town to isolate itself so thoroughly in this day and age? By ensuring that nobody cared enough to give it any thought, let alone visit it or move there.

Soon, she thought, it would vanish from maps altogether, just like Garland William Stevens's archives had been lost for so many decades. Maybe the roads that ought to bring people here would start to lead in different directions; satellites passing overhead would record endless days of cloud cover. Then perhaps someone might slip through, stumble upon it just as she had found Stevens's writings; perhaps that someone would find himself or herself unduly obsessed with a town that did not by any reckoning exist. But how long could you stay real yourself when you were devoted to something that only existed in liminal spaces? She wanted to ask Marisol if she was still real; she wanted to reach across the space between them and grasp her hand but the gap was too great. The light went to green and then back to red, and if Marisol was speaking to her, she could not hear her any longer, but she could hear their hymns, strange melodies with stranger words, calling to her, and she did not know how she came to be out of the car and walking up the middle of the abandoned state highway but she knew at last where she belonged.

She had driven out to a few of the Eudora quarries, once or twice a long time ago. Bored country kids from nearby counties used to go swimming there. They told her it was such a long jump that you had to point your feet downward so the soles of your feet didn't smack the water below, otherwise you could hurt yourself; but then they were all warned off going there in the first place because it was said there were dangerous things below the surface, abandoned equipment that could injure or kill you as you plunged deep underwater. She never swam there herself; she was too afraid of the depths, and you did hear stories from time to time about kids disappearing. The drop from the edge had always looked endless to her, and surely the water and whatever else lay below was endless as well.

She had always been afraid of the depths, along with so many other things, but now the fear was gone, replaced by something for which she had no name, because the depths were singing to her, and the sky yawned above, a black expanse trembling with stars. She walked down an abandoned highway, down a muddy red clay lane, down corridors lined by locked doors, down deep; she would walk as long as she had to, until they came for her, or until she came to them, for it was only a matter of time now, and she knew they would be waiting for her, in the depths, under the surface of things, and in all the places where it was dark.

*Virtually nothing is known about Stevens, and it has even been speculated that he was the invention of a collection of pulp writers at the time, including perhaps H. P. Lovecraft, Clark Ashton Smith, Donald Wandrei, Frank Belknap Long, and Robert E. Howard. Framer is the only scholar who—ostensibly—attempted to delve deeply into the life and work of Stevens. Unfortunately, it was later revealed that much of what she published about him was fabricated. There is no record that a town called Eudora, where she claimed Stevens was born and spent his entire life, ever existed, and certainly not in the location she identified. Framer herself, like a character from one of Stevens' stories, disappeared in 2015 without a trace.*

*– The Dictionary of Weird Horror (2019)*

# So Much Wine

She said, as they were falling asleep, "What does Christmas mean to you?"

He—wanting more than anything not to say the wrong thing, and having no idea what that wrong thing might be—bought time by replying, "Um."

Her voice was slurred with encroaching sleep. "I'm serious. What?"

Caution to the wind, then. "Mostly that Handsome Family song."

"What?" she said again. Then, "Who's handsome?"

Was she talking in her sleep? "The Christmas Day one," he said. "She wrecks Christmas because she drinks too much."

No answer. If she wasn't asleep before, then she was now, and that was good because he'd already said too much.

*December 14*

He said to her, point-blank, "Are you a ghost?"

She laughed and laughed. That didn't prove anything.

"Aren't ghosts supposed to be," she said, "you know, all, 'wooo'!" She waved her arms around.

"Wooo?"

"White sheets and . . . and chains? They have chains, don't they? Wooo!" She imitated—something, arms out straight in front, swaying from side to side, walking stiff-legged.

149

"That's not a ghost," he said. "That's, I don't know, Frankenstein. Or maybe a zombie."

"*Was* Frankenstein a zombie?" she asked. "A proto-zombie, maybe?"

For a few moments, they both pondered.

"Anyway," he said. "You still haven't shown me that you aren't a ghost."

"I so have," she said. But she showed him again anyway.

It still didn't prove anything.

*December 16*

Stephen started a list when things were slow at work. He started it on a piece of paper, not his computer, because everyone knew nothing you put on a computer was private, and he hadn't had his job for very long and didn't want to get in trouble.

At the top of the list, he wrote: "Reasons Martina Might Be A Ghost".

Then he wrote: *1. She is very pale and thin.*

That was a joke (kind of, it was also true), but he sort of had to work up to the real reasons he was making the list.

*2. She appeared out of nowhere.*

Sort of true. In the sense that she hadn't been there, and then she had. The Dying Dolls gig had been winding down, he'd had a little too much to drink and had been staring off into space. Someone had told him to go see the retro-goth band but they'd been terrible, campy and off-key, and he was in a bad mood at the end of it. Suddenly she was there where no one had been before. *Like* she appeared, but probably not *really*.

Stephen reminded himself that he was trying to brainstorm. That meant he wouldn't dismiss any suggestions out of hand. Later, he would look over his list and determine what was and was not sensible, but for now it was important to turn off the critical part of his brain.

*3. She has nowhere else to go.*

*I mean*, said the part of his brain that occasionally sent him little pep talks, little jolts of encouragement, *maybe she likes being with you. Maybe she doesn't* want *to go anywhere else.*

"They're renovating the apartment below mine," she'd said, more than once. "God, it's so loud. They start at seven A.M. Bang! Bang! Bang! And they keep fucking up other things in the building, like last week I didn't have hot water for two days and another time the electricity was off. It's just so much nicer to stay here."

No one would ever call his place nice, a bedsit at the end of a bus line in a shabby Edwardian house. He'd moved in after a disastrous run in a shared house in Dalston, but the place was dark and cramped and dirty and smelled off and his commute time was appalling even on a good day. The bedsit's main selling feature was an *en suite* instead of a shared bath.

"Don't you want to go home and get some clothes or something?" he'd said. Didn't she have plants she needed to water or post to check?

"Are you trying to get rid of me?" she teased.

"*No!*" Too vehement. "No, of course not. I just wanted to make sure, you know, you're comfortable."

"Afraid I'm going to stagger out into the street half-naked and claim you've kept me prisoner here?" She saw his face. "It's a joke, silly!" She lifted up the bedsheets, invitingly. "Besides, what do I need clothes for?"

She was right.

*4. Does it matter?*

*December 17*

"Hey, Stephen, we're heading out for a drink after work. You coming?"

It was a Thursday-after-work tradition. The question was a mere formality. Of course they were heading out for drinks; of course he was coming.

He thought about Martina, alone in the flat. Maybe she was bored or lonely.

"I have to—" he said.

"What?"

"Nothing," he said. "I'll be there."

Stephen had started out at the job as a temp. Even though they'd taken him on permanently three months ago, which meant that he was well-liked and was doing a good job, he felt his position there was precarious, and even though he wanted to be a writer and not a receptionist, he worried about the precariousness because you couldn't live on writing, especially not things he did, little horror stories that occasionally appeared in small-press publications and netted him twenty-five pounds if he was lucky, if they bothered to pay at all. Also, it was weird to be a male receptionist, even though you weren't supposed to think things like that nowadays. Stephen remembered a Swiss guy he'd met in a youth hostel a few years ago when he was backpacking through Europe who described himself as a "male nurse". Stephen was never sure whether it was a language thing or what. He imagined describing himself to people as a "male receptionist".

He stayed later than usual at the pub that night. He kept saying to himself that he would have just one more and then he would go, and he couldn't understand why the longer he stayed out the more reluctant he felt to leave. At the end of the night there was no one left but him and a guy named Will, who he didn't even like, and a girl from another department he didn't know. He thought they were probably going to hook up and that they wished he'd left ages ago. He was disappointed when his bus ran right on schedule. When he got home the apartment was dark. Martina had gone to bed. As he slipped under the sheets she drew him to her.

*December 18*

Actually, he knew Martina wasn't a ghost because she had a job. Or at least, there were job-shift-length stretches in which she was gone from the apartment, and she'd told him the name of the place where she tended bar. If she were a ghost who had to duck out for certain stretches of time, for whatever metaphysical reason such a thing would be necessary, surely she would have picked someplace where he would be unlikely to try to visit her while she was at work.

Which was exactly what he decided to do, at a loose end on a Friday night. Some friends were getting together at someone's house but it was all the way over in southwest London and some others were meeting at a pub relatively closer, but it would be weird not mentioning Martina and at the same time he didn't know how to explain it. "Yeah, it was at the end of the Dying Dolls gig. I dunno, she's kind of moved in with me." He could imagine their concerned expressions. There was also a woman from Tinder he'd been sort of seeing, and it was the same problem. She'd texted him a couple of times during the week and he hadn't replied, not knowing exactly what to say. That made him the kind of person who ghosted on people, which he tried really hard not to do. He told himself he'd figure something out in a day or two and text her back.

Anyway, the truth was, he kind of liked having something that nobody knew about. Not that Martina was a some*thing*—the something was everything, the whole thing they had going. Whatever that was. He liked that it was away from everything else, like a little secret world he could enter away from worrying about his job and his life and if maybe he was just a really shitty writer and he was destined to work crap office jobs for the rest of his life and be alone. He liked that it kept him from thinking about Amanda, or the Tinder girl for that matter.

So he headed over to the place in Shoreditch where Martina said she worked. It was in a weird area, kind of dark and out of the way. The place had been one of those old divey London establishments and then had closed altogether, only to be reinvented as a craft beer bar. He said he'd heard of it when she told him the name, but he hadn't. There were fairy lights in the window, but he wasn't sure whether they were for Christmas or were there all year round.

He went in. The interior was austere, long tables and benches instead of chairs. The bar looked like it was made out of green plastic. He was staring at it, trying to work out whether it was some hipster affectation or the owner just didn't care before he realised there were three or four people behind it and none of them were Martina. For a second he felt a mix of triumph and relief—she wasn't real; she'd been lying to him all along; he had a reason to end it, to kick her out, and then he saw her picking up glasses and carrying them back behind the bar. She hadn't seen him yet. He watched her for a moment or two. She said something to one of her co-workers, a tall tattooed white guy with thick black dreadlocks. Everyone behind the bar was tattooed except for Martina. In fact, every inch of Martina's skin was entirely clear of blemishes: he had never seen anything like it. Not a birthmark, not a mole, not a small scar from a childhood accident or anything. It was like she was made of porcelain; he imagined that if he tapped her too hard she might crack.

He'd had a nightmare about it, actually—one he'd forgotten until that moment, that he had found a crack in her leg, near her knee, and had traced it up and over her body and it had got wider and wider as he moved up, until there was nothing but a great black maw where her face should have been.

He was shaken on remembering it, and for a moment actually felt faint. He would add that to his list of reasons she might be a ghost.

Except all that was blown away by a new list, "Reasons Martina is Not A Ghost", starting with: *1. Ghosts don't have jobs.*

In that moment, she saw him. He couldn't quite read the expression on her face, but he thought it was safe to say she didn't look pleased.

She didn't go over to him or anything like that, leaving him to make his way to her. It felt like a long walk, those few steps from the door to the bar. "I thought I'd come by and say hello."

Her face was blank, almost as though she didn't know him. "I am at work," she said.

"I—yeah, I know that. I, uh, came to your work."

"I can't talk to you," she said, and stepped back from behind the bar, went back to collecting glasses.

All in a rush, he wondered if it was something to do with an ex-boyfriend—someone abusive, maybe, that she was on the run from, who would erupt into a jealous rage if he saw them talking together? He looked around the bar, but there were just groups and couples talking, no one glowering in a corner like he wanted to beat the shit out of him. A co-worker, maybe? But they were all occupied as well, appearing entirely disinterested in whatever was going on between Martina and him. Really, it was almost as though he was the ghost.

He wanted to go over and say something to her, even if it was just, "Sorry, I'll go," but something about her body language, the way she held her shoulders, kept him from doing even that.

That night, he waited up for her. She didn't come.

*December 19*

She did not come.

*December 20*

She did not come.

*December 21*

This was getting ridiculous. If the boyfriend hypothesis was true, she could be in trouble—injured, held captive, even (he did not want to think it) dead. He imagined that for a moment. If she were dead, it would be his fault.

But—if none of those things were true, he still needed to get in touch with her, because she had the key to his apartment. He'd given it to her on day three, since he was going to work the next morning. He hadn't wanted her to think she had to go home. Best case scenario was some random girl out there had his key; worst case scenario was her crazy ex-boyfriend had it and was coming to kill him. Either way, he was pretty sure the landlord wouldn't appreciate it if he changed the locks on his own, never mind that he couldn't afford it anyway.

His phone made a noise, a WhatsApp message arriving. For a moment his heart did a little leap until he remembered they had never exchanged numbers—they hadn't needed to. For all he knew she didn't even have a phone.

He picked it up.

*Fuck you, I thought you were different. Don't bother replying, I'm blocking you.*

The Tinder girl. He felt bad for a moment. He imagined her sitting round with all her friends, their levels of indignation rising. In his head, he defended himself to them: *I'm not like that!* but it wasn't the Tinder girl or what he imagined her friends' voices to be that responded. Instead, it was Amanda. *It doesn't matter how you think of yourself. What matters is what you do.*

On his lunch break, he rang Amanda from a work phone because he figured she probably had his number blocked, and if she didn't, she would as soon as she saw it was him calling. Instead he got a message about the number no longer being in service. That felt even worse than being blocked; at least if he was blocked, he still felt like she was out there somewhere, living her life. This way, it was like she had vanished from the world altogether.

Once he'd had the thought, he couldn't let it go. What if she needed him? The next-to-last time he'd seen her, she'd said she was doing really well. She hadn't looked like it— there had been dark circles under her eyes, and somehow her face had looked drawn even though it had also been bloated. She'd stopped drinking, she'd said. Completely. He'd made some noises at her—he hadn't known what to say, what would have been the wrong thing, how to come across as approving without being judgmental or—worse—altogether disbelieving.

And then there was the last time he'd seen her. Well. That didn't bear thinking about.

When he got home and pushed his key into the lock, he knew something was different, although he could not say what; in that way that your senses pick up on something before you can articulate it. He opened the door to the sound of a clatter of pans. Martina was making noise over by the cooker.

"You like roast chicken?" she said.

"I—sure I do." He noticed she'd bought a small Christmas tree she'd placed on the table in the corner. There were three rectangular boxes of varying sizes under it though the largest was only big enough as one that would hold perhaps a pair of children's shoes.

"I brought Christmas," she said with a grin, and he didn't bother to tell her he actually hated Christmas, or ask where she'd been or why she'd come back. He didn't care about any of it. He just desperately needed to feel her touch him again.

Later, they lay naked on the bed, the chicken on a platter between them, tearing at it like animals. He'd never seen the platter before either—meals in his tiny room tended to be more of the Pot Noodle or takeaway variety, so she must have bought that as well. "I always like some meat after a good fuck," Martina said. She had never cooked for him, so he wondered whether she always served meals this way. He tried to remember seeing her eat, and realised he hadn't, and wondered why he hadn't thought that was weird. *I like some meat after a good fuck.* Maybe none of the other fucks had been any good? He also wondered whether they should talk about what happened at the bar, but he was afraid to bring it up. And he wondered when he would have time to work on his novel again. It had occurred to him at work that day that he hadn't touched it since Martina had come to stay, and that maybe her leaving was a good thing. She had taken his mind off Amanda, sure, but she'd also taken his mind off everything else he'd planned to do. It was almost like he'd been in the grip of some kind of drug. Cold turkey, everything seemed so much clearer to him.

He tried to make his voice sound casual as he said, "So, I'm going to be doing a lot of work over the next few weeks. On my novel."

She nodded at him. She was lying on her side, elbow out, propping her head up with one hand and holding a chicken leg in the other, gnawing on it. There was grease on her face. All at once he was repulsed by her. He wanted her out of his apartment that moment, although he could hardly say *that*. So he gestured at the Christmas tree instead.

"And I'm leaving," he said. "First thing in the morning. I'm going to my parents' for the holidays. So thank you for the Christmas stuff, but I won't be around for it. Do you want to take it with you?"

She lowered the chicken leg, her face a picture of genuine puzzlement. "Take it with me where?"

"When you go. Tomorrow."

"I am not going anywhere, Stephen. You are the one who is going somewhere. You just said so."

"But." He was flustered. "You can't stay *here*."

"Why not? Are you afraid I'm going to try to rob you?" She said it playfully, but there was an edge in her voice. He wondered if it had been there all along and he was only now noticing. "I could come with you," she said. Her voice was neutral, but he felt her watching him carefully.

"Don't you have plans for Christmas?" he said.

"Yes," she said with a smile he would have described in one of his stories as *coy*. "I'm spending it with you."

*December 22*

His phone said it was five in the morning. He lay there for a long time, listening to Martina's regular breathing.

The problem, of course, was that he wasn't going anywhere. He wasn't even sure what, if anything, he was doing for Christmas. He and his parents hadn't talked about it. He had tried not to think about the holiday barrelling toward them at all after what last Christmas with Amanda had been like.

He wondered where Martina was from. She had the hint of an accent, and that along with her name had caused him to assume that she was from somewhere in Eastern Europe, which was to say practically anywhere. He thought she had said Poland once, but maybe he was misremembering.

He got up and put the light on. Martina, snoring softly, lay with her hair spread across the pillow. She had the covers pulled up tight. She looked so small, almost childlike.

Stephen put the kettle on. The water boiled, he made himself coffee, and still she didn't wake.

Six came, and seven, and still she did not wake. He took a shower, got ready for work.

Finally, he shook her.

She stared at him, bleary-eyed.

"I have to go," he said.

"That's all right," she said, and pulled the covers up around her head.

"Wait," he said, and stopped her, grabbing the top of the duvet and then letting go a moment later. He didn't want this to turn into a physical altercation.

He cleared his throat. "You need to leave," he said.

For a moment there was silence. Then, from under the duvet, muffled: "What?"

"You need to leave," he said again.

Silence again. Then, the duvet cover flipped back. She was laughing.

"I'm serious," he said.

"Don't be serious, Stevie!" she said, and though she tried to make it sound light, it was strained. Also *Stevie*.

"Don't call me that," he said.

"Why not, *Stevie*?"

"Look," he said, and he picked up her clothes, jeans and a jumper, and thrust them at her. "You need to go."

Her face changed. He saw it happen—not like a shift in emotion, but as though a mask had dropped—to reveal a different mask. Her true face, he sensed suddenly, was still

160

hidden to him. Several masks deep. Or no mask. No face. That maw from his dreams.

"Why are you doing this to me?" she said.

"I—look, I just want you to leave."

She punched herself in the jaw.

"What are you doing?"

She said, "Look what you did to me."

A bruise was already forming.

She thrust off the duvet, and she started pummelling herself in the same way, hard, mercilessly. The worst thing about it was that she did it so silently; tears forming in her eyes as she sat there naked and beat at her breasts and thighs and tore her hair out in clumps and all the while no noise at all.

"Martina, stop it!" He grabbed her wrists and she kicked at him, kicked him in the balls. The world went white and then red. He sank to the floor. When he lifted his head again, she was holding one of his kitchen knives. The nice one that Amanda had given him last Christmas before the day had gone well and truly to shit.

He tried to keep his voice steady. He pretended he was acting in a film, and he said the kind of thing he'd heard people in films say in these kinds of situations. "Martina, put the knife down."

She plunged it into her thigh.

As she fell back on the bed, shrieking, as her blood flowed onto the sheets, as he scrambled for his phone to dial 999, all he could think was how relieved he was that she had used the knife on herself and not on him.

There were police, there was an ambulance that took Martina away in it. One of the police, a woman, was a few years older than him. She was blonde and actually kind of attractive if, you know, police were your thing, which in Stephen's case they were not.

Stephen felt she had it in for him. From one standpoint, he couldn't blame her: they had one battered, bloody woman and one bloke. Usually it didn't take crack police work to figure out what was going on in a case like that. But—much to his surprise—Martina must have told them the same story he did, because they made him repeat it a few times, and they came back to him and followed up on some details and when they asked him who she was, the first time and after that, he said, *I don't know, her name is Martina. That's all I know,* and he saw the policewoman and a policeman, who he guessed was her partner, exchange a look but he couldn't read it.

*Family emergency,* he told his work, which was code for wadding up his bloody duvet and sheet and pillow, and finding the mattress underneath stained with blood as well, and thinking he was going to have to buy a new one and wondering how he would afford it.

He called a locksmith that afternoon and had him change the lock on his door. He would hash it out with the landlord later.

Later still he dragged out his old sleeping bag and killed what was left of a bottle of whiskey he'd been saving for Christmas while lying on the floor and not sleeping all through the long dark night.

*December 23*

He went to work the next morning.

It sounded so simple, said like that, but in fact it was anything but. He finally had slept, for an hour or two, and woke cold and stiff. He showered with the door open but still couldn't shake the feeling that she had somehow come back while he was in there, that he would walk out of the bathroom and she would be sitting there with the wound in her thigh spurting blood and no expression in particular on her face, just looking at him.

He stood for several moments with his hand on the doorknob of the flat, afraid to turn it. What if she was in the hallway? She couldn't possibly be, of course; she was in no condition to be out and about even if she'd been released from the hospital, which he doubted. He opened his door at last with a feeling in the pit of his stomach as though he were about to step off a roof and plunge to the pavement below, but outside was just the landing and the stairs. She was not on the next landing, nor in the foyer. She was not outside.

It was as though she had never been.

The office felt unreal in its mundanity. For the first hour or two he was on tenterhooks, waiting for someone to mention the incident he'd been involved in, as if such a thing would ever get reported in the news. By midday he was in the breakroom with a cup of tea, allowing the bland routines that normally infuriated him to soothe him instead.

It had been an awful experience, but it was over now. Whoever she was, she'd been a troubled woman. Time to move on. And maybe start looking for somewhere new to live. Not (he told himself) because of anything to do with her but because it had all just highlighted what a bad idea it had been to move to a shithole in the back of beyond in the first place, just like everyone had said it would be. He would start asking around about renting a room somewhere closer in.

It wasn't good for him, this living on his own. Not like this anyway, where it could take him literally hours round trip just to meet up with friends. It wasn't healthy, especially not after the year he'd had.

He scrolled through his Facebook notifications. He hadn't been on in a couple of weeks—since he'd first met Martina—so the site had resorted to sending him random notifications of only peripheral interest save for the news that someone had just tagged him in a photo. "Someone" because the name was written in an alphabet he did not recognise: it did not look like Cyrillic or Hebrew or Arabic or any other alphabet he was used to seeing from time to time on the site but the photo was on his mate Jez's page and was the two of them with two others, Paul and Mark, out at some pub. They looked wasted, him in particular, blearily raising pints to the lens. He tried to remember the night, who had made the photo. It was posted on 10 December but that couldn't have been when it was taken because that was the night he'd gone alone to the Dying Dolls show and met Martina.

Stephen clicked on the name that had tagged him but he was directed to an empty profile page: the same strange alphabet for the person's name but no photo, no friends, nothing at all.

It had to be some kind of weird phishing or hacking attempt—he couldn't think what it might be—but they were always one step ahead of you, weren't they? He remembered the night well, now that he thought of it: they had started near Jez's place in Bethnal Green and ended at some place in Hackney Downs that Jez had said he'd love. That was where the photo had been taken. The pub had some kind of occult name. The Wicker Man. The Hanged Something. The Hand of Glory. That was it. He *had* loved it, it had that whole folk horror vibe going on.

Stephen put the phone down and rubbed his eyes. He was getting confused: hadn't it been about a week and a half ago, when they'd been there? It must have been the night before then, but that was Thursday, he'd been out with his work mates as usual.

He picked his phone back up, scrolled back up through the messages:

*Right, on my way . . .*

He'd sent that on the Friday. Okay, so maybe the Dying Dolls gig had been on the Saturday. He went into his calendar. The Saturday was as blank and featureless as his memory seemed to be. He googled "Dying Dolls", got hits on how to dye your doll's hair.

He must have got their name mixed up. He tried different combinations: got Dresden Dolls, Death in June, New York Dolls, something called the Dead Doll's House in Islington. Anyway, he remembered the Saturday now as well: sleeping in, and later a party at someone's house, a friend of Mark's he didn't know well. He'd felt ill and left early.

"Drinks tonight?" said someone.

He looked up, confused. "But it's Wednesday." It was someone named Claire or maybe Clarisse or maybe something that didn't start with Cl— at all. She had dark hair that sort of fell all around her face and someone had said to him once that they thought she fancied him but he didn't think so.

"Right," she said, "but as tomorrow's Christmas Eve, we thought we'd do it tonight."

"Yeah," he said, "yeah of course," and he tried to say it casually but he heard how it sounded which was anything but, except that she didn't seem to notice so maybe it had been? He looked back up and there were holes where her face should have been. He shut his eyes.

"Are you okay?"

"Migraine aura."

"Oh shit," she said. "My mum gets them."

He nodded, eyes still closed, not caring about Cl-whatever's mum. After a few moments he thought Cl-whatever must have moved on but then he opened his eyes again and she was still standing there, staring at him.

"It takes a while," she said.

"What?"

"After the aura. It won't come right away. My mum gets the headache an hour or so later."

"Can you take the phones for a little while?" he said.

"I don't know if there's anyone here who can take over for you this afternoon if you have to go home. Half the office is already on holiday."

"I need to go," he said, and stood up, knocking his chair over. As he did so, he knew he would not be returning, and knew that would mean losing this job that he needed so very badly, and knew that there was nothing he could do about any of it. He stopped to grab his coat and his bag and he ran out of the glass doors in front of his desk, ran to the elevator, mashed its buttons but could not wait and instead took the stairs, two at a time, until his foot caught on one and he almost tumbled the rest of the way down. Only then did he slow, walking the rest of the way and pushing the door open and stumbling out into a day that was already cloaked in winter dusk.

The journey home was interminable.

The migraine never found him, but the police did.

The policewoman did at any rate. She was waiting outside the house where his bedsit was located. He thought about crossing the street and walking on past, but she spotted him at nearly the same moment and anyway it wasn't like they didn't know where he lived.

She said, "It's come to mine and my colleague's attention that you were interviewed after the disappearance of another girl around this same time last year."

He barked a little laugh. "Amanda didn't disappear," he said. "She left me. She fucked off to Ramsgate with a musician the last I heard. I never talked to the police."

The policewoman pulled a steno pad out of her front pocket. She started flipping through it, ripping pages off and discarding them on the street, which seemed entirely irregular to Stephen. When he looked, the writing on them was the same kind of alphabet he'd seen on the name that had tagged him on Facebook.

"That's not what our notes say," the policewoman said.

"Your notes are all over the pavement," he said to her, and then he thought he better not say anything else without getting a lawyer.

"Have you ever heard of a psychopomp?" the policewoman said.

*December 24*

The flat smelled: the carcass of the chicken he and Martina had eaten, still in the rubbish, and old, stale blood. He hadn't imagined any of that. Of course he had not. The little plastic tree was still there as well, along with the three gifts Martina had placed under it.

The encounter with the policewoman had left him shaken a day later. She was the one who had clearly lost it, not him, and he wanted to report her, or whatever it was you did. He suspected whatever kind of investigation she thought she was carrying on was unsanctioned by her department but he didn't want to draw any more attention to himself than was necessary.

He sat on the edge of the bloody mattress and drank a little water. He told himself he was glad he had changed the locks, but really it felt more like being trapped in there. He should get out. He should ring one of the guys, see what they were doing later on.

He did not do any of the things he thought about doing.

*December 25*

Christmas morning was cloudy and dark and cold. He'd forgotten to go to the shops, so there was only a bit of bread and no butter or coffee or tea. As he chewed on a piece of dry toast, he reached for the smallest of the three boxes Martina had left him and started to unwrap it.

Could a box feel alive?

*I only stopped in to give you your present. I couldn't return it and I couldn't use it myself, thought I might as well.*

Amanda had stood at the door of the flat they'd shared, the one he was going to spend New Year's Day moving out of because he couldn't afford it on his own. It was only midday but she was already swaying from side to side and he could smell booze coming off her, like she'd started the day before, or even earlier, and hadn't let up. Like she was soaked in it. Her hair wasn't combed and her eyes were red. She was still beautiful, but she looked terrible.

"You should come in," he said. He'd only mean to help her, give her a coffee, make her eat something and maybe get a shower and some sleep, and first she said *no*, and then *well maybe*, and finally she was in, across the threshold, and this was his chance to make it all right again.

He'd opened the gift she'd handed him, a small rectangular package. Inside was a chef's knife. He didn't know much about cooking, but it was heavy and shiny and so seemed like it would be expensive.

"Amanda, I don't know—" he said, and then, "Thank you," because anything else seemed rude, but when he looked up she'd swigged down most of the wine that he'd just opened, straight from the bottle.

"I don't know why I got you that," she said. "Stevie." She'd called him that affectionately once and later mockingly.

"I like it," he said. "Really. Maybe I'll actually learn to cook properly now."

She started laughing. "I think I hoped you'd use it on yourself," she said. "Stevie."

A year later, his hands shook as he pawed at the package Martina had left behind. She'd used too much tape on it and in the end he had to get up and get scissors. When he finally got the paper off, he found a clean, white box, and inside the box was nothing at all.

The same was true for the second, slightly larger package. It occurred to him that it was like a shop display: fake tree, fake gifts. Fake girl. All for show.

*Give me back the wine*, he'd said to Amanda, *you've had enough to drink*. He'd put the knife down and told her again to give it back. She was laughing still, leaning back on two legs of the chair and he lunged at her, not to take the wine from her (he thought) but to pull her back to safety, because she was drunk and she was going to fall. And then she did.

He had never in his life heard a sound cut off so abruptly as Amanda's laughter was at that moment, as the chair tipped over backwards, as her body, ragdoll-limp from too much drink, didn't even react in the long moment it took for the chair to fall, as the back of her head smashed against the hardwood floor.

The wine bottle didn't break, but the wine ran everywhere, like her blood.

*Well what would* you *have done*, he had asked the voice in his head that had reproached him frequently in the year that followed. *You don't know what you're going to do unless you're in a situation like that.* He had not gone to her. He had not called 999. He had not done either of those things because he was sure she was dead, she had to be, with all that blood. If she was dead, it did not matter whether he acted quickly or not. What he had done then was run out of the flat, slamming the door behind him (he'd had enough presence of mind to do that, at least), out of the building and onto the street, where that same winter dusk had cast a gloom about the entire city that the Christmas lights couldn't penetrate. He had run a long way, only realising after some time that he didn't have his coat or his wallet or even his keys and so when he did eventually make his way back he had to ring buzzers until someone let him in.

He braced himself before entering the apartment.

It was empty.

There was still blood and wine everywhere; but there was no Amanda, who had apparently not been dead at all but just knocked out, possibly concussed, and definitely never speaking to him again. Because whatever crimes they had committed against one another in the year leading up to that moment. There was nothing quite like knowing that when you suffered what might have been a deadly injury that the reaction of the person who loved you most in the world was not to try to get help but to run away. It would have been funny if it hadn't all been quite so thoroughly awful.

Stephen picked up the last box.

And he *had* loved her. More than anything; more than he had thought possible. Up until then, he'd honestly thought what he'd heard about in songs and seen in movies was just fantasy, and that when people talked about love, they were just riffing on that fantasy, that none of it was real, nobody felt like that, and yet with Amanda, for Amanda, it had been. Only none of them went far enough—it was more than a *feeling*, so much more than an *emotion*. It had been far more visceral and far less pleasurable, as though she were some vital part of him, not even an arm or a leg, but lungs or a heart, so that even when he didn't like her, even when he hated her, she was a part of him and would always be, and nothing either of them could ever say or do would change that. Even if he never saw her again.

His hands shook as he tore at the wrapping on the last box. What would he find inside? A lock of Amanda's hair, a photograph of the two of them together, a mourning portrait of Amanda on the floor, her eyes closed, her hair tangled with wine and blood? When he finally got the wrapping off it, he sat for a moment with the box on his lap before gingerly lifting the lid.

Like the others, it was empty.

Stephen swore and threw the box aside. Fucking crazy bitch. Both of them. And the policewoman, and him too, working himself into this state, imagining all kinds of things, imagining reality bending in on itself.

On impulse, he rang Amanda again, the same number as before, and as before, a recorded voice said the number was no longer in service.

Stephen went to the window. Outside it had begun to snow, big fat swirling flakes that almost made the street outside look pretty. He suited up, coat again, hat and scarf and gloves, and he went out, purposefully this time, not the way he'd left the old flat a year ago, fleeing. Only a few cars passed, and no one was out.

He walked for a long time. He came to a vacant lot where, from a distance, a huge black shadow appeared to move on the white snow like a living thing. When he got closer he saw that it was a flock of crows that took flight as he approached, and he thought of the words of the policewoman: *Psychopomps*.

After a time the snow changed to rain, and then back to snow again. The dirty winter dusk gave way to night and the clouds parted and the sky blazed with more stars than seemed possible to see in any part of London, and still virtually no one was out. It was almost like a city of the dead. That wouldn't be so bad, he thought, if it just snowed and kept snowing, the drifts rising higher and higher, and soon the trains couldn't run and the planes couldn't land and all of Britain would eventually fall asleep, all its problems forgotten; soon the island itself would be lost to the world— soon it would be a ghost like all the others, like Martina, like Amanda, like himself, surrounded by a wine-dark sea and frozen at the heart.

## An Element of Blank

The call came late. Sabrina had just managed to get Bea to sleep after hours of trying, and she swore at her carelessness in forgetting to turn off the ringer. As she scrambled to mute it, she saw the familiar area code but did not recognise the number. She didn't need to. Bea, miraculously, slept on as Sabrina stepped into the hallway and pulled the door shut behind her. She knew without knowing. She said, "How did you get my number?"

Mandy was startled awake by the phone and for a few moments she did not know where she was; even as she came to herself, she still could not say with certainty. She'd blacked out a few hours and a lot of drinks earlier. Everyone said that was a warning sign, which made Mandy laugh. She could tell you a thing or two about warning signs.

There was someone in the bed that was not her bed, and this was not her room, not her apartment, and she was stumbling naked around some strange man's bedroom swearing and looking for her phone so that it would not wake him and, of course, waking him in the process.

She found her purse near a crumpled pile of her clothes and as she was fumbling for her phone opened her mouth to apologise and realised she couldn't remember or had never known his name. The apology died on her lips anyway as she saw a number flash on the screen, an unfamiliar number but with an area code she knew well. She didn't care who she woke anymore, or about anything else, as she said, "Why the fuck are you calling me?"

It was two A.M., Cora sat in the dark where there was nothing that could scare her. The phone calls had gone about as well as could be expected, which was to say not well at all. Now it was just a matter of waiting until they arrived. She had done all she could for now, and she told herself that, but it didn't feel like enough. There had certainly been nothing heroic about making a couple of phone calls, as difficult as they had been. There would be nothing heroic in the days ahead, either. They weren't thirteen-year-old girls any longer, driven by a childish sense of adventure and invincibility.

Cora did not believe in destiny, but sometimes you made decisions that set you inexorably on a path that you could never leave. She and Mandy and Sabrina had done so nearly three decades ago. Now the end of the path was in sight, and they could no more find a switchback or set off in search of a different path than a train could leave its tracks. She tried to think of it objectively, as a thing without malevolent purpose: it was like being exposed to a carcinogen that lurked in your system for decades before blossoming into cancer. You were fated to meet that end and no amount of healthy living or right choices in the interim could make it any different.

She wondered what the other two remembered. She wondered about the accuracy of her own memory; time had a way of distorting even the clearest of recollections. She had done some reading on the study of memory, and what she took away was that memory was little more than lies. The human mind had a way not just of colouring or reshaping the past but of making it up whole cloth. Happy childhoods became horror shows. Trauma rewrote itself into something bearable. People even took bits of other people's memories or scraps of stories they heard or television shows they saw and wove them into their own recollections, believed those stories to be theirs. The most intimate part of you was a liar, and it was impossible to even tease out which parts. You weren't who you thought you were and neither was anyone else. It was a monstrous way to live and it was the only way humans knew how to be.

Like the old story of the blind people and the elephant, once they were together again they would each describe their part and try to make sense of the disparate pieces they had carried with them for nearly three decades. For herself, she remembered the smell of sulphur and decay; the void where his eyes belonged; the terror that washed all the colour from the world.

*Red Rover, Red Rover, send Cora right over.*

That was the game they played as children. And Cora would go, she would run, not as fast as Sabrina, and certainly not Mandy, but of the three of them she was best at breaking through the chain of children on the other side.

*You forgot to say, "Mother, may I"!* That was another game, and a rule that always eliminated the others, but Cora never forgot. A mind like a steel trap, her own mother used to say.

She had always been the best at games. And at remembering things—which meant she did well in school, effortlessly—but there was so much she had forgotten. She hoped the others would help her remember.

Mandy was the first to arrive. Cora watched her get out of her car before stepping onto the porch to greet her. She looked older than in the carefully curated public Facebook photos Cora had seen of her, older and tired. They all did, probably, and more so in the last forty-eight hours. Mandy's blonde hair was pulled back in a slack ponytail and she was wearing jeans and a stretched-out black t-shirt that looked like it had been slept in. Cora felt a pang of guilt; maybe she had done the wrong thing in summoning them here.

But that was silly. She had only done what she'd promised, and she had neither the power nor the inclination to summon anyone to anything. Mandy and Sabrina had made the choices they did from their own free will.

That was if you accepted that they *had* free will. Cora was unsure.

Mandy didn't say hello, or how have you been, or wow, it's been twenty-something years. What she said as she turned to Cora, as though no time had passed at all, was, "Sabrina . . . "

"She's on her way. She's had to arrange child care. She's got a new baby." Cora saw Mandy's expression. "It's her wife's," she said. "I mean, it's both of theirs, but she's not the one who gave birth."

"Still," Mandy said. "She shouldn't have done that."

*I will follow you forever. I will pursue you in every creature that you ever dare to love.*

It was almost as though Mandy had the wrong idea about all of this, as though she thought anything they had done mattered. As though they were going to come back on the other side of it and return to their normal lives—as if anything about their lives ever had been or ever would be normal.

Mandy said, "Well, my boss thinks I'm out of town for a family emergency. Hopefully we can get things wrapped up before that excuse runs out."

Cora said, "Mandy, what do you remember about that summer?"

## An Element of Blank

1988. Sabrina's Bangles and INXS cassettes on constant repeat. It was a hot Georgia summer like all the others. They were thirteen years old and best friends since first grade: the three musketeers, Porthos (Mandy), Athos (Cora), and Aramis (Sabrina). They referred to one another by those names when they were around others to confound them.

They read all the time and passed what they read between themselves—not just *The Three Musketeers*, but *The Diary of Anne Frank*, and Trixie Belden, and the Babysitters' Club, and the Dark Forces horror novels for kids, and Stephen King, which Mandy snuck off her mother's shelf because her mother said the books were too scary and too grown up for little girls.

"We aren't little girls," Mandy said solemnly, and they weren't. They were in that dangerous wilderness that was neither childhood nor adulthood, pulled in both directions and belonging to neither. And all in different places: Sabrina, dark-haired, the one adults always called beautiful, looked closer to eighteen than thirteen, and had a boyfriend that she kept a secret from her parents because he was already old enough to drive a car. Mandy was tall, thin, and tomboyish, the best at sports, a track-and-field star at their junior high and thus courted by nearly every single coach at the high school they would attend in the fall. Cora loved watching her run, because she always looked like a beautiful wild creature, her long blonde hair streaming behind her.

Cora-then thought of herself as the ordinary one, the steady, smart, quiet one, the one (she was sure) boys would never notice and mothers would always love. In books, girls like her grew into beautiful swans or were compensated for their lack of beauty and charisma with exciting careers. She thought she might become a palaeontologist, or an astronaut, or a marine biologist.

Cora now distrusted nostalgia. Not just because her own life and the lives of those she loved most meant that there was damned little for her to be nostalgic about. It was, for her, inherently suspect, an indulgence unconnected with reality. And yet she could not help dividing their lives in two: years that were washed in a golden light, when the three of them were growing into who they were *meant* to be. A beauty, a jock, a brain, but so much more than that, because they were human, not types, and they laughed among themselves about how they knew others saw them, that their peers and teachers thought they were all so different from one another and wondered at their peculiar bond, but what they knew was that their hearts were the same, they were practically the same girls under the skin, closer than sisters. They loved each other with an intensity that only children could muster, before their egos and senses of isolated selves had entirely emerged, when they still believed that they could really stay together forever.

Cora knew that golden light wasn't real. Like everything about memory, it wasn't to be believed. What memory and sentiment burnished was merely ordinary at the time; they were ordinary girls, living ordinary lives, but wasn't that what was so wonderful about it? When things became extraordinary—that was when it all went wrong.

What happened to them—what happened to them was random, in the end, and that was one small part of what was so horrible about it. That was one of the horrible truths about life in general—its randomness, the way the most unfathomably terrible things happened to people in the blink of an eye due to whatever collection of happenstance placed them in harm's way. Sprayed by the bullets of a crazy man at the mall because you stopped in to order an Orange Julius. Snatched by a child-killer because you lost sight of your mommy in a crowded store. Dead on a roadside because you'd driven at just the right speed to meet a driver whose car slipped across the centre line at just the wrong moment. Sinners in the hand of an angry god, indeed.

Or maybe not; maybe not so random. Not for them, anyway.

It had been her idea. She would never forget that, and the others would never see it that way: three musketeers, all for one and one for all, and stalwart to the end, they would insist it had been all of them who caused it to happen, not just Cora the instigator. But she had always thought otherwise.

It had seemed like fun. They had imagined they were setting out on an adventure. A real haunted house! They would spend the night there, using the time-honoured round robin trick of telling each parent they were spending the night at another's home. Cora's mother had been the wild card— the one, in fact, who might have saved them. She had a habit of phoning round to other parents to make sure an overnight stay was in fact permitted, but this night she had slipped (almost as though it was meant to be, almost as though the thing in the basement of the house were manipulating events for its own purposes, but that didn't bear thinking about).

They had not needed to break in. Cora had been the one who had discovered the way in at the back, that the door seemed locked, but if you leaned on it in a certain way, and moved the knob up and down in just the right manner, it opened for you, or it had for her. This, too, she had come to find suspect over the years. But at any rate: the house had opened for her.

The Idlewyld House. It had been abandoned forever, or at least for as long as the girls had been alive—same thing really—before that, it had been lived in for five or six decades by a reclusive old lady, a widow who had hidden herself away from the world when she was very young, on the death of her much older husband sometime in the 1920s.

Cora had loved the house, a sprawling monstrosity
that had seemed unable in the end to make any sort of
architectural commitment, spanning the styles of Gothic and
Victorian as well as antebellum plantation. The Idlewylds had
been transplants from Europe. Idlewyld had not been their
real name, but she could not find out much about Gerald
Idlewyld's true origins. What she did learn she shared with
Sabrina and Mandy till the three could scarcely contain their
excitement. She read to them from the notes she had taken:

"Gerald Idlewyld, magician, warlock, acolyte of Alistair
Crowley, Golden Dawn adherent until he argued with
founders and left the group, and aging heir to a fortune in
Scotland, married a girl a quarter his age, Catherine, seventeen
to his nearly seventy, and said to be so beautiful that every
man who saw her fell in love with her. She had been interested
in none of them though; in fact, her only aim in life before
she met Gerald Idlewyld had been to enter a convent. Three
months after their marriage, a private affair attended by no
one including the family that disowned Catherine, they were
driven out of his ancestral home and fled here, to Winston,
Georgia, where no one knew them . . . "

"How did you find *out* all this stuff?" Mandy asked, her
eyes wide, and Cora explained to them about the magic of
interlibrary loan, plus her mother had been pursuing a degree
part-time at the university an hour away and Cora had taken
to accompanying her to campus when she could, spending
hours poring away at her little research project in the library.

She could not remember when she had first become
fascinated by the house. It was fair to say she had always
been drawn to its soaring turrets, its gargoyles glaring from
the rooftops, its schizophrenic design. Most of that had been
added by Gerald Idlewyld; it had been a typical antebellum
mansion when he bought it. "He went all Winchester
Mystery House on it and started building rooms on rooms

and sticking weird things all over the outside like those gargoyles," she told the girls. The townspeople had hated it, but it violated no zoning laws. When Catherine Idlewyld, the young wife who had grown old and mad living alone in her husband's house, finally died, some people had thought this was their opportunity to tear it down, but it had been bequeathed to some mysterious foundation back in Scotland, and so still there was nothing they could do.

Cora had only discovered by accident that there was a way in, and she had not entered on her own then. She had not wanted to. Instead, she wanted to share it with Mandy and Sabrina: all three of them so loved stories of adventure, and she would bring this adventure to them.

And so they had all turned up at dusk, sleeping bags stuffed into backpacks along with snacks and cans of Coke and flashlights and notebooks and a tape recorder, and they stood at the door, and Mandy said, "You should be the one to go in first, Cora," and so she was.

After that, unreliable memory became very unreliable indeed.

Sabrina, spread-eagle on the floor, blood vessels bursting in her eyes until they turned red like a demon's, black bruises blooming on her flesh like patches of rot, screaming for them to get out—

Sabrina, after they'd dragged her out with them, vomiting till there was nothing left in her stomach, then just dry-heaving, staring just past them like she could see things they couldn't, asking them, *Why did you bring me out?*

Because of the three musketeers. Because they were Athos, Portos, and Aramis, and that meant all for one and one for all. No matter what.

"He'll come for us," Sabrina had insisted. "If you had left me it would be over now. You didn't and now he's going to keep coming for us. He won't stop. He never stops."

They had tried to finish the summer out as though it had never happened: going to the skating rink and the city pool, slumber parties, bugging Sabrina's mom—the only one who didn't work—to take them to the movies or the mall. Going to the library, which they still loved, even though the summer reading program had seemed too babyish for them for a couple of years now. But none of it was right; none of it was real any longer. The only real thing in all the world was what they had awoken in the basement of the house, that thing that had them in its grasp and lost them and so had pursued them that night and all across what was left of the summer, and all the days of their lives.

Cora offered to make Mandy something to eat, but Mandy said she wasn't hungry, and so Cora brewed some coffee instead. "I hardly ever eat an actual meal really," Mandy said absently. "I can't remember the last time somebody cooked me something. I wouldn't know what to ask you to make for me." She was looking round with an expression Cora couldn't read.

"What is it?" Cora said.

"Just—it's weird to be back here. Your old house. But you've always been here. I don't mean in a bad way," Mandy hastened to add. "But it brings back memories."

Cora shrugged. "Someone had to stay here." Then she felt bad, because it sounded like she was accusing Mandy of running away, which she hadn't meant. "So tell me about yourself," she said by way of making up for it. "The non-Facebook version."

Mandy smiled sadly. "Facebook, well, you *have* been thorough. Let me see. Three ex-husbands, probably an undiagnosed mental disorder or two—the exes were all

182

certainly ready enough to call me crazy—and constant self-medicating with a variety of legal and illegal substances. You?"

Cora shrugged. "Celibate, overeducated, and chronically unemployed. Diagnosed with clinical depression that's proved impervious to whatever my doctors and I throw at it. I tell my doctor there's no medication that can treat having looked into the mouth of hell. He thinks I'm being metaphorical."

That broke the ice that neither realised had formed in the room. They both burst out laughing and could not stop. They sobbed with laugher; their stomachs clenched; they laughed until they couldn't anymore, and of course they couldn't. Who could, what normal person would? There was nothing funny about any of it. The laughter died away and left a bigger silence in its wake.

"Sabrina's the only one of us who turned out okay," Cora said at last. "How did that happen? She was always the wild one." Sabrina had been not just the first to have a boyfriend but the first to have sex, get drunk, smoke weed, take drugs. By the age of sixteen she'd seemed bent on a life of self-destruction. And here she was now a respectable married lady with a baby and a wife.

"Maybe that's why," Mandy said. "Maybe because Sabrina was always just herself, and feeling exactly whatever she felt, and damn whoever got in the way of her at any given moment. Maybe she worked it all out somehow."

They sat, and considered the implications of all that, and neither of them said anything further for a very long time. Then Mandy said, "How did you know? How did you find out that he was back?"

She had told both of them over the phone that she would explain when they arrived, and they took her at her word. They took her on faith. Faith was something all three of them had very little reason for any longer, and so she was moved that they trusted her in this way.

She said to Mandy that at first she had not believed it herself. She had existed in a kind of stasis all these years, waiting for a thing she both knew and yet could not quite imagine was going to happen.

First had come the dreams, but that had not been definitive. The dreams had plagued her for years, and she assumed that was the same for the others. That the dreams intensified was disturbing, but not in and of itself indicative.

Next, though, there had been the incident on the road. Cora dutifully took classes at the same university where her mother had studied and where she herself had first embarked on her study of Idlewyld House. Sometimes community extension courses—she had a smattering of education in a dozen foreign languages—but she poked away in a desultory way at a bachelor's degree in physics now and again as well. In a different life, a life that had excluded that one night, she thought she might have become an academic instead of a poorly-paid bookkeeper at a local trucking company who told herself she was keeping her mind fresh by taking courses in programming and differential equations and quantum mechanics.

She had been driving home after a night class, and was on the long rural stretch of road outside of Winston. She had stopped at a train crossing, and sat idly as the freight cars rushed past, thinking about nothing in particular, maybe about the soothing sound of the train and its whistle, maybe about the dative case in Russian. It didn't matter. What mattered was that she didn't know how long she sat there, that suddenly she became aware that the train had long since passed and that she was sitting there still, window rolled down to take in the night air, the engine off, the sounds of cicadas, the soft wind, and something else. The digital clock on the dash told her it was midnight, which mean that she been sitting there for well over two hours. Two hours of lost time. She had never experienced such a thing. Fear sent a cold trickle down her spine. Why had no one stopped for her? Anything might have happened to her. Anything at all, and she could not remember a moment of it.

She sat there in stark contemplation of this fact, and then she reached for the ignition, but as she did so a pickup came bumping over the tracks in the other direction and a teenaged boy wearing a baseball cap poked his head out of his own open window.

"Ma'am," he said, "are you all right?"

"Yes," Cora said, "yes," head down, trying to start the car—why the hell wouldn't it start? Why was it making that awful grinding noise over and over?

"I just asked," the boy said, "because you know after I went around you a few minutes ago, I got to thinking and got worried about you. Maybe because how you just didn't seem like you reacted at all to me blowing the horn at you, but more because of the guy in the car with you. Sorry, ma'am, if he's your husband or something."

Cora said, "What did you just say?"

"The dude in the car with you. Where'd he go? Are you sure you're all right?"

Cora couldn't speak. She wanted to say I'm all right, I'm fine, wanted to get away from this boy with his innocent probing questions, she wanted to drive forever and wake up somewhere and somebody else.

"You need a jump?" the boy said. "I got cables in here."

Cora twisted the key in the ignition again. To her surprise, this time the car started up smoothly. "I'm fine," she said. "Thank you, I'm fine."

"That guy," the boy said. "Is he—"

She never found out what the boy thought that guy might be, because she pressed on the gas and was away, as though she could flee him, someone who had been sitting there next to her, and her insensible for hours. *Someone*, she thought, as though who it might have been was some sort of mystery.

*One-two, buckle my shoe. Three-four, shut the door.*

Shut the door, Cora! Shut the door!

But Cora hadn't.

*Five-six, no more tricks. Seven-eight, an endless wait.*

That's not how the nursery rhyme goes. But she'll be damned (and she will be) if she can think of the right words.

*Nine-ten, I'll see you again.*

Four little words. Four little words of the kind that are spoken between lovers forced to part, between bosom friends, between parent and child. Not words for him.

*I'll see you again.*

*Not if I see you first*, they'd say, and laugh because it was stupid.

*He saw me first.*

That night, she did not sleep. She sat up in her living room, lights blazing, all the faucets turned on because she had once read that witches could not cross running water. She went to work the following morning in a fugue state, and he was everywhere, hiding in the spaces between words people spoke to her, entwined in the numbers she added up in long columns. He could do that, fold himself into the substances of things and wait for as long as needed. She went home that night and spent hours steeling herself for the phone calls she knew she would have to make. It was very late when she finally forced herself to do so. She wanted to weep because the sound of their voices reminded her of how very different it all should have been, but she thought if she wept he might see her. He could find his way in through tears.

186

She told Mandy most of these things. Afterwards, they sat in silence waiting. They told themselves they were waiting for Sabrina. Secretly each knew they were waiting for him.

But it was Sabrina, after all, who found them first. Sometime after dark she came hammering at Cora's front door. She dispensed with formalities, just as Mandy had: no, how have you been, the years have been good or bad to you, only that she was sorry, she'd come as quick as she could. Sabrina was as beautiful as she had always been, maybe more so, even though her thick brunette curls had been chopped into something short and sensible, and her face was drawn with the exhaustion common to new parents. Cora tried to remember what she'd found out about Sabrina, that she was a manager at some kind of software start-up, a modern type of job for a forward-thinking person and a billion miles away from a lich in a basement, a story of possession, an occult nightmare. The very existence of a Sabrina seemed to preclude the existence of a Gerald Idlewyld, and yet here they were.

Cora said she'd put more coffee on to brew and Sabrina asked why.

"I thought we'd have some while we talk about what we should do next," Cora said.

Sabrina shook her head. "There's nothing to talk about," she said. "We know what we have to do, and time is on his side. The sooner we act to finish what we started, the better."

Cora knew Sabrina was right even as she protested. But Sabrina persisted. This wasn't a social gathering. There was no time to reminisce, not even for the type of reminiscing that they told themselves was preparation for a battle. There was no preparation they could do that they had not already been doing for the past twenty-five-plus years. Anyway, while they were sitting around preparing, what was he doing? Getting stronger every second.

As Sabrina went on speaking, Cora saw that she was prepared to die. Of course she was; they all were; wasn't it what they were here to do, after all? She wondered what on earth Sabrina had said to her wife and her baby daughter.

Maybe *I'll see you again*. Nine-ten. Did Sabrina recite nursery rhymes to the baby? Cora thought not; if there was one thing all of them knew, it was that nothing, least of all nursery rhymes, was as innocent as it might appear. Counting rhymes and games in particular were tricky. She had become a bookkeeper because she thought manipulating numbers might save her, but she was always looking for him, lurking beneath a string of zeroes. An infinity of nothing. One of the most terrifying things about magic was how it turned science to its advantage.

Mandy said, "Should we drive?" and Cora said, "No, let's walk." She knew instinctively that it had to be as similar as it had been the other time, and she almost suggested that they bring well-stocked backpacks along. But Sabrina was so impatient she knew there was no point in bringing it up.

"How did you manage?" Mandy said. "Living here all these years with that place nearby."

Cora said, "I never went near it again. I haven't been past that street since that night."

That wasn't entirely true—every few years she forced herself to go back by the house, to stand outside and look at it and remind it that she was coming back—but it was near enough to the truth.

They set out down the sidewalk, crossed Tate Street, walked up toward the old fairgrounds and took a right.

*Step on a crack, break your mother's back*, but her mother was already dead, dropped from a heart attack eight years earlier, just the way she'd have wanted to go, not a single day of illness or infirmity to speak of from the day she was born until the moment of her death.

Now left, and past the Chinese restaurant that had, according to the sign in its window, been "Closed for Renovations" for years now. *One-two, buckle my shoe.* Back to that again, then. *One-two, guess who.* No need to play a guessing game. *Three-four, open the door.* That was where they had gone wrong: opening the door that ought to have remained shut forever.

Sabrina grabbed her right hand and Mandy her left as they rounded the corner onto the street where Idlewyld House stood, hard unloved survivor that it was. "All for one and one for all," they all said, under their breaths, and they went forward.

"It looks the same," Mandy said. "How does it look the same? Does somebody look after it?"

Cora said, "I think it looks after itself." She herself could scarcely bear to lay eyes on it, and it was hard to remember that it had once been an object of love and fascination for her.

The house looked unprotected, which didn't mean that it *was* unprotected, far from it. They went round the back of it and there was the door, it must have been a servant's entrance, and just like it had before, it opened at Cora's touch. It had been waiting for them.

The act of stepping across the threshold was a shocking one. She remembered very little of any of this: what sorts of things they had seen inside the house, whether they had gone from room to room, whether there was grand furniture covered in sheets or whether it was empty. She didn't even remember the basement, really, nor what had drawn them there in the first place. So she had nothing to compare it to, but what she stepped into this time at least was not a house, but a long, dim corridor, one that stretched as far as the eye could see.

*Come closer*, something said. *Send Cora right over*. And, as if an afterthought: *Red Rover, Red Rover*.

It had that way about it, of getting inside your head. She reached again for the hands of the others, but she seemed to be alone. Not only that, but she was sure that she was thirteen years old again, that the years had fallen away. You always were thirteen years old, a part of you anyway: all the ages you'd ever been stayed inside you, locked in along with the memories.

Catherine Idlewyld must have told herself that, curator of the memory and legacy of her husband, as she grew older and madder.

*Red Rover, Red Rover*, the thing said again. It was forming itself out of bits of Cora's memories. Cora tried to shut it out. But she couldn't help herself: *Mother, may I?* she asked.

There came no response. Cora set off down the corridor, one careful foot in front of the other. She felt things crunching beneath her feet and she looked down to see that the corridor was paved with bone. She was starting to remember things she had learned before, the last time she was here: flesh was sacred, all material was holy because it was all made of ancient stars and dead universes. All those saints and mystics and magicians who prized the spirit over the mind had it wrong. It was on the body that the secrets were inscribed, not the soul. Gerald Idlewyld had got it wrong as well. There was nothing special about being dead. Most things were, after all. But to be alive—to be alive, or to have been alive—that was so rare, and so brief, and so strange, when you considered it, to come into physical being, such chance, almost mathematically impossible—

Math held some of the secrets, and the rhythm of rhymes, and the games children played that had their origins in sacrifice and death, and sacred numbers, like three, three little girls, a holy trinity of flesh for the dead, only one little girl was far more clever than any little girl ought to be. Sabrina—

Not Sabrina. It came to her all in a rush, how memory had tricked her yet again, not Sabrina, but she, Cora, had been the one they'd dragged from the house that night. She had been the one who'd fought off the ancient demon thing that had called itself Gerald Idlewyld. She had known without knowing, and it was why she had been the one who remained here to watch all these years. Had the others known? Surely this was his doing, for if she could not remember, she could not know her own power, and he might stand a chance of defeating her a second time, and of making his way into the world again.

He had imagined her weak and vulnerable then, and he had been wrong. Then he had infected her memory, but he was wrong again. And finally, he had been wrong to separate her from the others. He had thought it would weaken her further, but it meant they could not carry her away this time.

She remembered all the rhymes and games meant to keep out devils; she knew numbers better than he did and how they explained the universe; sacred flesh met evil spirit and a conflagration occurred.

Later, witnesses said the old Idlewyld house literally burst into flames. No one was sitting and staring at the house, of course, at the moment that it happened—no one who reported it, that is—but they heard the explosion, saw the fireball rushing up toward the sky. The house was engulfed in minutes.

In all the excitement, two women nearby would have gone little noticed, and if noticed, would have been thought part of the crowd of gawkers that had quickly gathered, and nothing to do with the freak accident that spelled the end of the house that the town had hated for a hundred years.

As for Sabrina and Mandy—they could think only of their Athos, lost to them for so many years, found briefly, and now gone forever: either of them would have gladly taken her place, if they could have. All for one and one for all at the end of the end of it all.

Mandy had a new lover, a nice one she had met through a blind date arranged by a friend, and she was trying to moderate her drinking these days. She had phoned Sabrina once or twice and left messages for her that Sabrina did not return and Mandy had come to realise that this was for the best. She increasingly felt that her own memories could not be relied upon and that it might be even more distressing to speak of them to Sabrina, so she left her alone.

Sabrina and her wife had a second baby, this one borne by her, a little sister, Cora, to now two-year-old Bea. Cora was still a beet of a baby, red and almost too tiny to be believed. She was a brave baby. It seemed a strange thing, perhaps, to say of a newborn, but it was true all the same. Sabrina could tell.

Her wife had asked her about the name. It was an odd choice, she'd thought, an old-fashioned name, but Sabrina had been so insistent about it. She'd known a Cora once, a Cora who had mattered to her a great deal although she could no longer say why. Memory was like that. Fallible. Unreliable.

*An Element of Blank*

She liked to play a game with Cora and Bea even though they were both too young for it: *Red Rover, Red Rover, send Cora right over*, she'd say, and she'd chase Bea down with Cora in her arms and Bea would squeal and giggle and demand that she do it again and again.

If she dreamed, fleetingly, of a house with gargoyles that crawled among its many chimneys, or of a woman whose flesh annihilated a demon, or of the cleansing power of fire, they were only passing dreams, and they did not linger. In fact they failed to encode themselves upon her synapses at all, and so at dawn it was as though they had never been.

193

# The Seventh Wave

## I.

*D*o you know the story about the girl who walked into
the sea?
    *Did she drown?*
*No, she didn't drown. They pulled her out.*
*That's good.*
*No it's not. It was the worst thing in the world they could
have done.*

I want to begin this story in this way: I have always loved the
sea. But then I stop and I think: which sea? There are so many
of them. There is the sea of my childhood: the flat blue glass
of Florida's Gulf Coast, the dirty ocean off Galveston Island in
Texas. There are the seas of my later years, the freezing Atlantic
smashing against the shores of western Ireland, the windswept
grey waters of the Oregon coast outside my home right now.
And there are the seas of my imagination, the seas I read about
in books and never saw, or saw and was disappointed by so
that the sea remains forever extant only in my memory. There
is the sea of the Greek isles, a sea I somehow always thought
would indeed be *wine-dark*, but was not. There is what I think
of as the Gothic sea: it is somewhere off an English coast,
surrounded by cliffs and moors and castles, with family secrets
and brooding men lurking. This sea, too, does not exist except
in my mind. Then we have the metaphorical sea: we can be all
at sea, which is bad, or in a sea of love, which is good, I guess.

194

But my story is about the sea, and about love, and it is not a good story at all. Or rather, the story itself is a good one, I suppose, if you are not in the story, because the things that happen in it are very bad indeed.

Because I am old, and because tonight I *feel* old, and because it is forty years to the day from another, terrible night, I am going to set down here the story of myself and the sea, and all that it took from me.

Every thing and every person that I ever loved taken from me.

## II.

*Do you know the story about the girl who walked into the sea?*

Women and men have been throwing themselves at death on account of love for as long as there have been humans and some concept of love, or maybe for longer: when I was a child, I had a dog who mourned the passing of its mate by refusing food for so long it nearly died too. Before our not-yet-human ancestors were capable of the kind of planning that hastening death requires, they probably still starved themselves, or lay out in the elements, or let themselves get eaten by sabre-toothed tigers rather than bother trying to carry on.

Anyone who isn't terrified of love is either a fool or has no idea what it means. For myself, I'd sooner be flayed alive than fall in love again. You might say there is little chance of either of those things happening. At four score and five I am supposed to be preparing to die, but not from love, and certainly not from *la petite mort*—just from ordinary decay. At my age, the capacity for that quickening of the heart and the spirit and the loins is supposed to be long gone. And yet it happens. It happens to those my age and even those older than me, the ninety-year-olds, the hundred-year-olds. The human heart is never too old for passion. It is the very young who believe otherwise, but then, the very young believe everything is for them and them alone. There is the old, true adage that every generation believes it has discovered sex for the first time: and yet there is no act, no position, no method of penetration or manner of stimulation or path to ecstasy or perversion that men and women have not been doing to one another in various combinations for at least as long as they have been dying for love.

I find this extraordinarily heartening. I wonder how different humans might be if we wrote history as a chronicle of significant orgasms rather than political intrigues, poisonings, betrayals, battles won and lost. I take a wicked pleasure in saying this sometimes to people because it shocks them. "*Abigail!*" they tut, or, "*Mrs. Brennan!*" if they are on less familiar terms with me, clearly believing I am one of those elderly people who has taken leave of my senses and is now just saying any old thing that pops into my head. And none are ever so shocked as the young. For all their posturing, the young really are terribly conservative, because they *are* so young, and so hopeful, and so they've yet to figure out that nothing at all ever really matters much in the end.

But where was I? I am old, you see, and I digress so readily. Ah, yes. The sea. The ghost story. Lost love. And the girl who walked into the sea, the girl they pulled back out again.

You may or may not have surmised by now that the girl was me, and if so, you are correct. Had they not pulled me out again, *I* might have been the ghost in this story. And a terrifying, vengeful ghost I would have been as well. I'd have smashed ships against rocks, rent sailors limb to limb, drowned swimming lovers. I was so consumed with sorrow and pain on the day I walked into the sea. Those things would have felt almost like an act of mercy to me, as though

I were doing those people a favour, showing them the true face of the world, and that at the end of it all there is only suffering and fear. Sparing them one more single agonising second of living.

Despite all this, it would, as I said, have been better had they left me there to drown.

I am certain as well that you do not need to be told *why* I walked into the sea that day: for love, of course. For the sake of a man. I was twenty-five years old, a late bloomer, as they say, but then I was possessed of a lethal combination of being both intelligent *and* unattractive. These days a woman can buy permission to be smart or talented or successful with good looks for as long as she remains young, at least; in my day, being pretty meant you couldn't possibly be bright while plainness was just an affront to everyone. By everyone, of course, I mean men.

I must have been almost unfathomably easy prey for Philip, the married man at the office where I worked who set his sights on me. (Philip, how funny to think of him now! He is either very old or, more likely, very dead. I cannot imagine encountering him now, doddering and senile.) In those days, for me, both virginal and naïve, he was the height of dashing sophistication. I had never even kissed a man, had presumed I would be a spinster my entire life, and as for sex, that was something I gave little thought to, and never in connection with myself. The result of all this was that a man I later came to understand was very ordinary was able to seduce me and convince me that, without him, my life was worthless. After two months of surreptitious rendezvous in his car, twice in the office, once in a hotel room (I told myself then he must *really* love me), he informed me that he had no intention of leaving his wife; two weeks later it was clear he'd taken up with the nineteen-year-old secretary hired a week before he dumped me.

I was, as I said, naïve. I had imagined that there was something extraordinary in what passed between us, in the pleasures of sex, that anything that seemed so intimate must surely *be* intimate. I was in love, though not with him— people say *in love with love*, and that's wrong too. I was in love with the man I thought he was, and in those short two months, I believed I was the best version of myself I have ever been although in fact I was alternately neurotic, terrified, giddy, hopeless, and consumed. Love can do that to you. And then it ends.

When it became clear to me that I had been no more than a passing fancy that he quickly tired of, I resolved to kill myself, both to send him a message and because I truly did feel that I would not be able to live with my pain. Better that he had cut me open and literally torn my heart from my body than this agony of drawing breath after breath. I did not yet understand how the most appalling pain can recede over time even if it never goes away. Time doesn't heal, but enough of it and it begins to tell us lies that let us live in the present, if we allow it.

*If the past does not come to you. Did you hear about the girl who walked into the sea? Did you hear what became of her children?*

The story of my suicide is routine and not very interesting. I did very little planning. In those days, I lived in Savannah, Georgia, where my family had moved in my teens, and so I drove to Tybee Island and found what I mistakenly believed to be a deserted bit of shoreline. Fully clothed in a skirt and a sweater and heavy shoes, I walked out into the ocean. Had I put more thought into it, I would have chosen a more reliably empty beach; I would have weighted my pockets to ensure I did not bob to the surface. I would have forced myself to drink the salt water into my lungs. That I did none of those things, however, was no indication that my suicide attempt was merely a cry for help. I was serious; but with suicide as with sex, I was a complete novice.

Novice that I was, I was spotted, and saved by a nearby fisherman. I spent two nights in the hospital, and I believed that Philip would come to me there, having seen the error of his ways. When he did not, I understood at last that I had been a very silly girl, and that I was no different from many very silly girls who had come before me. I quit my job and found a new one and resolved to stay far away from men for the rest of my days.

I told myself that I had survived not because of my rescuer, but because, as I loved the sea, the sea loved me back.

I have, you understand, been mistaken about love throughout my life.

Do you hear that? Some would say it is only the howling of the wind and the crashing of the waves, but I know the sound of my children's cries. I must move along and finish my story for you before they come for me.

### III.

I had sworn to stay away from men, but the revolving door of dull office jobs that were available to no-longer-so-young women in the 1950s eventually brought me into the path of an even duller man named Bernard. He was everything Philip had not been; where Philip had been charming and smooth, Bernard was awkward and fastidious. But he had other qualities. He was steady and dependable. And we did have one thing in common: Bernard loved the sea as well. The first time he took me sailing, I thought this was a man who would never betray me as Philip had, because there was no room in his life for another love.

And so it was that almost five years to the day after they pulled me from the sea, I walked down the aisle with Bernard.

No one could say that I had not done well for myself. In those days, I was considered an old bride, and fortunate to snag such a reliable man. Bernard's boring nature extended to the bedroom. I told myself I didn't care; with Philip, I had seen what passion got you. Having said that, it seems surprising to me to this day that we managed to conceive three children. I told myself I was content, and I settled into an unremarkable domestic life that was exactly the same as the content and unremarkable domestic life that most of my peers had as well. I no longer had to work or worry about the future.

But appearances deceive, do they not? Because then I met Clive, and of all the dull, content, settled people around us, I would have said that Clive was the dullest of them all. Not that I am making myself out to have been a remarkable specimen myself: my oldest child, Deborah, was twelve, and I had long since passed from young and unattractive into aging and matronly, or so I felt. Clive said that was not the case; he said I kept myself trim enough to pass for at least ten years younger and that any man who could not see the unkindled fires banked in me must be blind. But he would say that, wouldn't he? He said a lot of other things, too, things married men say in affairs, but I believed they were true: that Stella, his wife, was frigid and moreover didn't love him. I couldn't have been more different from her, he said, and what he meant was there was almost nothing I wouldn't do for him, and he was right.

He even begged me to leave Bernard. And I might have; I told myself that Bernard, preoccupied with sailing and his accounting work, would hardly notice my absence. We no longer lived as husband and wife; we hadn't slept together since before our third child, Joann, now six, had been born. We even had separate bedrooms. Because I had long ago proved myself to be a poor first mate, too dreamy by far, he hadn't taken me sailing with him in years. It was just as well. I was content to sit on the shore or wade into the shallows with the children. The truth is, I liked the sea less with the children along. There seemed so many more hazards with these tiny, vulnerable people at my side: stinging things, and big waves, and tropical storms and hurricanes, and the sea itself, always pulling away from shore, too eager to take everything with it. The idea of its unfathomable depths, which had once exhilarated me, had come to terrify me instead. I suppose you could say that motherhood made me dull but I would argue instead that motherhood made me *aware*. The world was so full of danger. It was a wonder any of us managed to navigate it for any time at all.

And the sea is terrible in other ways, haunted as well—by millennia of drowned sailors. By pirates and their prey. By captains and their passengers and their crew, by mercenaries and soldiers and lost explorers, by unwary fishermen and swimmers and beachcombers and people who did not notice the tide drawing in. The sea is heaving with corpses and dead souls. It is a stew of old bones and rotten flesh.

It is my single consolation: that wherever they are out there, my children are not alone.

But still they need their mother. All children need their mother, do they not?

I know what you are thinking. That they are going to be horrors when they come in from the sea. That the loving embraces I imagine will be grips of death. That they will be foul, decayed, mad creatures, that they will fall on me with salt-puckered eyes and mouths and suck the life out of me. Or that I am mad myself: old, and mad, delusional, that I ought to have been put into a home long ago, and that I need *help*. *Help you*, hang you, burn you. You are ugly, female, and old: three strikes and you're out, but you are worse, you are alone, you are reclusive, you are not kind and grandmotherly and comforting. Your eyes do not twinkle.

We are too enlightened to call you a *witch* but we will steal your life away from you anyway and lock you away and feed you drugs and call it a mercy.

So, you see, this is a risk I am willing to take. And what mother would not willingly give up her own life for her children's?

I would have, you know. What happened to them was not my fault. I couldn't have saved them. No matter what anyone says. I loved them and I lost them but I did not kill my babies.

## IV.

They say that you never really know a person, and they are correct. Case in point: my Bernard. I thought him incapable of passion, save for his love of the sea. I thought the children and I were little more than props in his dull life. I even thought he might be the kind of man to turn a blind eye to the fact that his wife had a lover. What did he care? He didn't seem to want me.

I was wrong. Bernard found out about us, not in a dramatic fashion. He didn't stumble upon the two of us in bed together or anything so crass. He saw a look here, a touch there, noticed an absence or two that could not be explained. He is an accountant, after all, and he added it all up, and he knew.

He need not have done anything. Ours was a business arrangement, I had explained to Clive, but a business arrangement with children involved, and as such, I couldn't think of leaving him, at least not until little Joann was off to college. It wasn't fair to either Bernard or me or to the children, who adored their father.

Why could that not have been enough for Bernard? Why could he not have allowed us to go on living with a small lie within the much larger lie that we were all living, the one that said we were a happy, contented family?

Even now, I do not believe what Bernard discovered inside himself was a passion for me, or for his family. There is a certain type of man who has a passion for the things he believes to be his. His own feelings for the things are not the issue; his ownership of the things is.

I do not know how long he was aware before he took action, but he did not give me any indication that he had noticed anything. One late-spring day, I went to pick up the children at school, only to find that none of them were there. Their father had come and taken them out of class in the middle of the day.

From the moment they told me, an icy lump of fear settled in my belly. *He knows.* I told myself it was something else, something innocent, but I knew better. And yet even then, the worst-case scenario that I could imagine was that he would divorce me and be able to keep the children, because what judge would leave children with an adulterous mother? And then Clive would abandon me as well, and there I would be, middle-aged, alone, unskilled, unemployed, a pariah among all who knew me and with no resources to seek out a new community. My parents were dead, and I had no family left. Where would I go? How would I live? *Why* would I live? What would be the point of anything at all?

I phoned Bernard's office; his secretary told me he was not in. I couldn't bring myself to speak to Clive. It was as though if I did not say anything to anyone, whatever was happening would not be happening, would not be true.

I sat there in our home and I waited. I didn't know what else to do. I didn't eat or drink anything. I didn't read, or watch television. I couldn't. I smoked, compulsively, one cigarette after another. It grew dark. And then I heard the sound of Bernard's car in the driveway, the doors slamming—

and the children's voices. I almost sobbed with relief. I had half-convinced myself I would never see them again.

They came tumbling in ahead of him, and immediately it was clear to me that they knew nothing was amiss; moreover, they'd had a fantastic day. All of them were sunburned and windswept, having spent the day on their father's boat, a rare treat, and they were all talking to me at once, and I started to think that perhaps I had been wrong. Perhaps Bernard had had a single unpredictable moment out of his entire life and decided that he and the children would enjoy spending a day sailing, with no ulterior motives or secret knowledge behind it all.

Then he walked in, and I looked at him, and I knew.

He said quietly, "Joann, Kevin, Deborah—go brush your teeth and go to bed. Your mother and I need to talk."

They all stopped short at the sound of his voice, and I remember thinking how much like wild animals children are. Their emotions are one with their bodies, and they had been so excited as they all jabbered to be heard above the others that they were contorting themselves, jumping up and down, making hilarious faces, all long brown limbs and sun-bleached hair and laughter. But at the moment their father spoke, everything changed. They were suddenly as wary and watchful as a deer who has sensed a hunter in a nearby stand. They froze; their eyes twitched; their mouths closed. They knew that of all the moments there had ever been, this was not one to argue.

They hugged and kissed me in a perfunctory way and left the room. At any other time, I'd have scolded Bernard for speaking to them so sharply and cutting off their joy. But I had no speech left in me. I had nothing in me.

Or so I thought. Until Bernard spoke, and of all the terrible things I had imagined in the hours leading up to this moment, I never imagined anything as terrible as what he said to me:

"I took the children sailing today so that I could murder them."

He let that sentence hang between us for a few moments before he continued. And as he did so, I thought some part of him was loving this. Meek, inadequate Bernard had the floor in a way he'd never had before in his life, in a way he'd never dreamed. I was as captive an audience as anyone could ever hope for.

"I thought it would be the best way to hurt you most. And it's still what I want to do to you—hurt you, as badly as I can, in as many ways as I can. I was going to go through with it, and I actually had Joann in my arms, ready to toss her over the side, and do you know what stopped me? It wasn't love of the children. I don't love them and have never loved them, and I want you to be very, very certain of that, because one of the things I want you to know is that your beloved children are going to grow up with a man who does not love them at all. I know how much that is going to hurt you. I think it might hurt you even more than if they were dead, knowing I am going to bring them up, poison them with lies against you, and loathe them because they are the spawn of such a filthy, deceptive creature as you."

He went on in that vein for a very long time. I do not remember for how long, or what all the things he said were, because it was impossible for me to move past that first point. *He was going to kill the children. He was going to kill the children.* And he had not done it today, but what was there to stop him changing his mind in the morning, or in a week or a month or a year? And what was this reservoir of pain and anger and hate that I had never seen in Bernard, who had never so much as raised his voice to any of us? Who was the man I had married?

Looking back, I suppose he was thinking something similar about me.

He kept on like that, haranguing me, and sometimes he would require me to respond, and I would, as best I could. I remember thinking that I had to keep him there, keep him talking, and morning would come and he would have to go to work—because surely he would not allow his routine to be disrupted for a second day in a row—and then I could do something. I didn't know what, but I had to do something. He didn't shout at me; didn't raise a hand to me; in a way he was still my mild-mannered, soft-spoken Bernard, and that was what made it all the more terrible.

Even the most awful things come to an end, and that night did at last as well. Bernard went to shower and dress for work and I went to wake the children for school. Their tired, drawn faces, so different from the elated ones that had greeted me when they burst into the house the previous night, told me all I needed to know about how much they may have overheard and understood.

## V.

My plan—I did not have a plan, or not much of one. I told the children we were taking a vacation and that Daddy would be joining us later. I do not think they believed me, but they knew something was wrong and they were too frightened to put up a fuss, although Joann did timidly ask me once if I was going to tell her teacher why she had missed school. She was only in first grade, and was still very excited about it all. I snapped at her, which I will always regret, and she retreated miserably into herself.

I left Deborah to oversee their packing while I went to the bank. I was terrified that Bernard would make or had made this stop before me, and so as soon as possible after they opened I was there to draw as much money as I could out of our joint account. I remember how troubled the teller, a lady named Mrs. Cook, looked as she counted bills out to me, like she knew that something was wrong. Of course it was; married ladies did not turn up alone and make enormous withdrawals without some cause.

I do not like to include this part, but I am trying to be as honest as possible here—I knew there was a chance that shortly after I visited the bank, Bernard might stop in as well, in the interest of vigilance, and find out what I had done. For all I knew, they might phone him and tell him themselves. And I knew that if such a thing happened, he would immediately go home, and all would be lost. This was my one chance, the only chance I would ever have for a decent escape. And so when I returned home, the first thing I did was to make sure that Bernard's car was nowhere in sight; the second thing I did was park my own some blocks away, and walk home from there. And the third thing I did was position myself near the window while the children finished gathering their things so that if Bernard did come home, I would have some warning; I would be able to flee, I would be out the back door and away up the street to my own car before he even realised I was there. I would make my getaway, alone. It was not what I wanted, but it was what I would do if it came to that.

I told myself this was the next best thing. I told myself this was better than being trapped here with the children, that the children would be fine without me, so what if they were taught to hate me, that my presence would make him more volatile and they'd be safer with him and they would be okay. They would grow up okay. They would never know how he felt, or didn't feel, about them. These are the lies I told myself to make it okay for me to abandon my children with their insane father if it came down to it, a choice between them or me.

Other women are not like this, are they? It's documented— it's why women stay in terrible marriages, in deadly situations, in order to protect their young or just to avoid being separated from them. I loved my children more than anything in the world; I loved them so much I found that love almost unbearable; and yet surely there is something wrong with me, that I could do this cold mental arithmetic that would permit me to leave them behind if I had to. But I am not a monster. I said it forty years ago and I say it here, again, I did not hurt my children. I would never hurt my children.

It was the sea, the ghosts, the dead things. The seventh wave.

## VI.

I didn't know what to do, so I just drove. The children were subdued. They knew everything I'd told them was lies. There was no vacation, there was no Daddy joining us later, and something was terribly, terribly wrong. That first day, I was so afraid that I drove for eighteen hours straight, keeping on back roads. I was sure that he would have reported us missing and that law enforcement everywhere would be combing the highways in search of a car of my description with my license plate number. But I was so exhausted that I began hallucinating—imagining people stepping out in front of us on the road—and I finally pulled off and paid cash for a motel room, pulled the car round the back, and piled us all inside where we slept.

We lived like that for a week or more—me, driving until I couldn't any longer and then a motel. I kept heading west. Isn't that where people go to reinvent themselves? I'd never been west of Texas or north of the Mason-Dixon line. I imagined the entire West Coast as a glittering paradise where we would be safe.

I bought spray paint to inexpertly disguise the colour of our car, and somewhere out in the desert, at one of the many low-end, no-questions-asked types of places where we'd spend a night or two to rest up, I asked a shifty-looking desk clerk if there was some way I could get a different license plate. I could barely get the words out; it was such an alien thing for me to do, but he reacted as though customers asked him for things like that all the time, and they probably did. He told me he'd have something for me when I checked out in the morning. After that I relaxed a lot more. Not only were we thousands of miles away from Bernard, but we could not be casually identified either.

Yet I still didn't feel safe. We got to southern California and I couldn't stop; it was as though movement had become a compulsion. I turned north, and we went up through the state and then crossed into Oregon and the Cascade Range. And then we were out of the mountains and by the coast, and it was a sea like I had never seen before. The sea I was used to was on the edge of hot white sands, and it was warm for swimming. This sea was icy, washing up on pebbled beaches or crashing against rocks and cliffs. It was grey and roiling. In comparison to the sea I was accustomed to, it felt wild and untamed.

And I finally felt safe.

Those days were such a blur that I don't know how long we were on the run for. Ten days, two weeks, three weeks? I have never known. But I thought, we can do this, we have done this, I have done this. We can disappear. We *have* disappeared. And I think for the first time ever in my adult life I felt a sense of exhilaration and possibility, that the life that had been written for me was not the one I had to live.

True, the children were disoriented and traumatised; they missed their father, and cried for him and for their lost home. But children are resilient. I would find us a place to live, get them enrolled in school in the fall, and things would be better. I still wasn't sure how I would find work or support us, but I had enough cash to at least buy myself a few weeks, and surely in one of these resort towns on the coast I could at worst get a job cleaning hotel rooms.

It was in that exhilarated spirit that we'd had an evening picnic on the beach. It had been windy, and a little on the cool side for our Southern bones, but the sun sinking into the ocean had been beautiful, and the children seemed almost happy for the first time since that evening they had come in from sailing with their father. They had begun to run about and play on the rocks jutting up from the water. The tide was actually on its way out, and the waves were choppy, but not nearly of a size to alarm.

I didn't actually see the moment it happened. I had turned away and was tidying up the remnants of our picnic, was thinking idly rather than in a panicky way for a change about what I would do the following day, that I would start to look for work, when I heard a piercing shriek—

And all of my children were in the water, and were being carried out to sea.

I ran in after them. I tried to save them.

You must believe me.

*They* must believe me.

## VII.

People tell a story in these parts about the seventh wave. It is not something I ever heard of in my childhood growing up along the southeast coast. The dangerous sneaker waves that snatch people to their death here do not exist where I come from.

Here, though, the ocean is crueller. These waves come out of nowhere, out of a placid sea. They say that every seventh wave is the one to watch out for, that it is the unexpectedly large and dangerous one.

I read about the seventh wave, all those years ago. I even called an oceanographer at a university here and talked to him about it. I was so distraught for so many years, and I felt that if I could only understand why it had happened, it would lessen my pain. What I learned was that science and superstition do converge, that patterns do exist in which roughly the seventh wave or thereabouts will be the largest. But sneaker waves lie statistically outside even this estimation. They cannot be explained. No one can say when one will rise like a great hand out of the sea and pluck people from dry land and drown them. No one can say why.

I do not know when, but I understand why. The gods and the demons and the ghosts that live in the sea demand human sacrifices. What could be lonelier than being dead? And down there in the ocean depths where pale eyeless things swim, beasts that are nothing but tubes and mouths lurk, where monsters that have thrived since the planet was young and all of evolution's nightmares converge under cover of darkness and deep, deep water, down, down, down they dragged my three babies, creatures of sun and light.

It is so late here. It is as late as the ocean is deep, as dark as the depths of the ocean and the blackness of space.

*But*, you say to me, *you say you love the sea. How can you love such a terrible thing?*

Have you not been reading the story I am telling you? Have I not always loved terrible things? My love has been nothing if not misguided and unwise. And how could I not love the sea, when my children are a part of it? No matter where I go in the world, I can touch the sea and touch some part of them, the atoms of their being.

On that day, twenty years after I walked into the sea in my attempt to die there, I ran screaming into the sea demanding that it bring back my babies. Ancient and implacable, it did not reply. And it was so calm. You'd have never guessed that such an act of inexplicable violence had just occurred.

Everything came out after that, of course: my flight with the children, and accusations from Bernard that I was unhinged and had killed them. Because of him, they investigated, but they said they found no reason to think that what had happened was anything but a tragic accident. Bernard said he would never believe that. I think it is because he had a guilty conscience. I would never have hurt them. What kind of a mother, what kind of a person would that make me? I am not that kind of person.

All of the publicity was strangely advantageous for me. A local innkeeper took pity on me and gave me a job cleaning rooms. From there, I worked my way up to supervising the maids, and then over to the front desk, and at the end of it all, I was running the inn. Somehow, from all that horror and despair, I made a good life for myself. I could never have imagined such a life.

And I travelled the world, and I visited the sea everywhere I went, and every year, on the night of my children's death, I walk down to the shore where it happened and I talk to them. I tell them what the last year of my life has been like and I tell them stories about how their lives would be now. The first few years it was easy, but the older they get the harder it is; I cannot imagine my babies, even little Joann, in their forties and fifties now! They would have families of their own, of course. Their lives would be blessed. I would have seen to it. I would have given them good lives. I would have.

This is the first year I am not able to go down to the beach and talk to them. The weather is too bad, and I have done something to my right foot that makes it difficult for me to walk. I am hesitant to see a doctor about it. I have remained what people call "surprisingly spry" throughout my older years, and I know how they are, these medical people, how they take one look at you and diagnose you with "old", and everything that comes after that is secondary to the disease of "old", and the next thing you know they are poking you and prodding you and trying to put you away, and you with nothing to say about any of it.

But I have a little house that is right on the coast, on the edge of a cliff with a path leading down to the shore, and I can hobble out onto my front porch and see the sea smashing against the rocks below. I don't dare go any further than that. This storm is very violent; it feels as though the wind itself could pick me up and toss me into the ocean. They *would* collude in that way, the elements, to get me back to the sea, to do away with me like that.

I have not gone out just yet, though. For some time now the wind has been howling in a way that sounds like the children crying. They are calling for me over and over: "Mother! Mother! Mother!" Children get so angry, and they must be disciplined. They must not be allowed to run wild and do whatever they like, don't you think? It spoils them, and above all, children must not be spoiled.

It's better for them this way. We saved them from love, saved them from passion, the sea and I. My only lover, my one true love, vast and unfathomable and savage, subject to the whims of the moon and the vagaries of the wind, oh my darling brutal sea.

Something thumps on the front porch. A single thin line of seawater has trickled from under the front door and across the floor to stop now at my foot. Their voices on the wind are so loud now, shrieking for me, and their little fists are beating at my door. My children have come home. Suddenly, for the first time, I feel afraid. *I never meant any harm to come to them.*

Can you believe that?

Will they believe that?

# Story Notes

## "The Dying Season"

Robert Aickman has been one of my biggest influences since I first read the astonishing "The Hospice" in my late teens, so I was delighted when writer and editor Simon Strantzas asked me to write a story for an anthology he was putting together called *Aickman's Heirs*. I wrote the bulk of "The Dying Season" in the exact place where it is set—an odd holiday park in the off-season in England, where I'd gone for a few days' writing retreat. There's something sinister in its banality, and that—along with the spirit of Aickman—inspired this story.

## "The Séance"

Although Anthea Wainwright is a painter, this story was inspired by the work of the photographer Francesca Woodman, a phenomenally talented artist who committed suicide at the age of twenty-two. Her work was macabre, grotesque, and criminally unappreciated in her short life and feels almost as though it has a strange occult power to it. I wanted to explore that in this story alongside another of my favourite subjects, unhealthy, obsessive love.

*"The Other Side"*

Joel Lane was a writer who meant a lot to me when I was sort of falling out of love with horror fiction in the mid-1990s. I discovered him and a whole host of British writers dubbed "miserabilists" at the time in publications like Stephen Jones's *Best New Horror* and the TTA Press publication *The Third Alternative* and fell right back in love again. I got the chance to meet him once, at the 2010 World Horror Convention in Brighton, and he was so generous and kind—as I gushed about how much his work meant to me; all he wanted to talk about was how my own writing was going.

I missed catching up with him at a convention a couple of years later, as you do, and assumed, as you do, that I would meet up with him again the next time, only of course, there wasn't a next time. Joel died, shockingly and prematurely, in 2013. I was very much moved, then, when Peter Coleborn told me that along with Pauline E. Dungate, he was putting together an anthology of work in which each writer would choose from among Joel's notes—a sketch, an outline, perhaps just a few sentences—and write something based on that. I was immediately drawn to the piece I chose, which became the letter that Adam sends to Mark in "The Other Side". It may be presumptuous to say it, but I felt quite close to him as I was writing it, and I tried to capture a bit of his spirit. I hope what I ended up doing with those notes is something that would have pleased him.

*"The Secret Woods"*

Anyone who loves Arthur Machen's novella "The White People" as dearly as I do will probably recognise that I'm drawing strongly on its influence in this story by the time they reach the fevered excerpts from Diana's journal. More than twenty years ago I wrote a novel that was eventually seen by at least half the agents and publishers in or adjacent to the genre of weird and supernatural fiction—it garnered a lot of rejections along the lines of "this is beautifully written, but also what the hell is it". The idea I'd originally had for it was riffing on "The White People" in a modern American South, essentially set exactly where I grew up. The same Machen story was of course also T.E.D. Klein's seminal text for *The Ceremonies*—which I'd loved but actually wasn't thinking about at the time—but unlike Klein, I wanted to get into the mind of the girl who wrote the journal. The novel was really an artistic failure, and in the end, Rosanne Rabinowitz did a much better job of evoking the woman's side of the story, this time from Machen's "The Great God Pan", when she let Helen Vaughan take centre stage in her novella *Helen's Story*, than I ever did in my novel.

I could never let go of the core of the story I wanted to tell, however, about a young girl bewitched and consumed by Pan, and when Mark Beech of Egaeus Press asked me for a story for a Pan anthology, I leapt at the chance to tell a version of that story in short story form. I like to think it succeeded where the novel failed; maybe it really wanted to be a much shorter piece all along.

*"Knots"*

The older I get, the more impressed I am by all the things that we really don't know about the way the world works, and this strange story unfurled feverishly from ruminations about the simplest physical properties that we don't understand. It's also a story about that thing that is most terrifying to many of us, or at least to me—loss of self. It can happen to anyone, but women in particular, I think, are vulnerable to losing who we are in relationships. And finally, it's about patterns, houses—another favourite subject—and the deep unconscious. Although to be perfectly honest, it's one of those stories I finished writing and first thought, "Where the hell did *that* come from?"

### "The Vestige"

In 2001 I took a strange night train journey from Bucharest, Romania to Chişinău, Moldova, and shortly afterwards, I scribbled down the opening paragraphs of this story. Over the years I tried to go back to it several times but could never get a handle on it. Finally, well over a decade after I began it, the story fell into place. It's not the first story I've written about the weird sense of dislocation, of almost being physically dissolved, that you can get from travelling to unfamiliar places on your own, and it almost certainly won't be the last.

### "The Unknown Chambers"

In 2012, I got an email from an editor in New Zealand, Lynne Jamneck, saying that she was working on putting together an anthology of gothic Lovecraft fiction with S. T. Joshi, and if it came together, would I be interested in contributing? I think I nearly broke my wrist in my haste to reply affirmatively; the chance to riff on Lovecraft in a Southern gothic way was too good to pass up. I'm afraid I did my own hometown—I borrowed its geography and industry—something of a disservice in this story, as it is not in fact populated by terrifying Lovecraftian spawn, but that's the danger of being anywhere near a writer, isn't it? I had so much fun creating the character of Garland William Stevens, writing his demented passages and inserting him into the history of weird fiction; perhaps I'll return to him someday.

### "So Much Wine"

This story was written for a Christmas issue of the excellent and long-running magazine *Supernatural Tales*, edited by David Longhorn. David and I have been friends since he accepted one of my earliest published stories, "The Last Reel", back in the days when almost no one seemed to want to publish me! The song "So Much Wine" by The Handsome Family is one of my favourites, although when I sat down to write this story I initially anticipated a slice of Americana; I didn't really expect it to unfold in the London setting as it so naturally did. I don't often write from a male POV but I really enjoy it when I do, and I particularly enjoyed, I suppose, exploring "the male gaze" in this one, the way that the women in it are such ciphers to Stephen. Perhaps only for me, it also ended up being a bit about the direction I felt the UK was taking at that point—and England in particular—in a kind of frozen, isolationist direction, although I hope it can be enjoyed without that particular baggage by anyone who is so inclined.

### "An Element of Blank"

This was another one written for David Longhorn. I explicitly set out to do a female response to Stephen King's *It*, a book I loved a lot when I was eighteen. It's still a book I love, I've just never gone back to re-read it! But over the years it raised the question for me of why there seem to be quite a few horror novels steeped in coming-of-age stories for boys but not so many about girls, *We Have Always Lived in the Castle* notwithstanding. I suspect one reason for the dearth is that King is so ubiquitous in the genre, and he does boys-coming-of-age so very well. I'd also had an Emily Dickinson poem scribbled down for years that I wanted to turn into a story, the first line of which is "Pain has an element of blank", and the poem goes on to one of the most poignant depictions of the all-consuming nature of emotional pain that I've ever read. I wanted to write about characters who were similarly consumed. This was the second of three stories in the book written at the same location, different time, as "The Dying Season" that I've used as a writing retreat over the years.

*"The Seventh Wave"*

This story was written for writer and editor Paul Finch's *Terror Tales* series. Most of that series is set in the UK, but this one was a bit broader, *Terror Tales of the Ocean*. This is the third story I wrote at the seaside writing retreat, and originally I intended to set it along that stretch of England's South Coast (with a bottle or two of Adnam's Ghost Ship Ale to keep my spirits up). I walked around for a day or so taking a load of photos for reference, but as happens with stories, it had a mind of its own and it ended up set next to the oceans of my childhood and the stretch of Oregon coastline that I lived near years ago. I remember that while writing it, the voice of the narrator was so powerful that I felt like this one was dictated to me; I only needed to listen to this tale that Abigail Brennan so desperately wanted to share.

# Sources

"The Dying Season" was first published in *Aickman's Heirs*, edited by Simon Strantzas (Undertow Publications, 2015).

"The Séance" was first published in *Uncertainties: Volume 1*, edited by Brian J. Showers (Swan River Press, 2016).

"The Other Side", based on a story fragment by the late Joel Lane, was first published in *Something Remains*, edited by Peter Coleborn and Pauline E. Dungate (Alchemy Press, 2016).

"The Secret Woods" was first published in *A Soliloquy for Pan*, edited by Mark Beech (Egaeus Press, 2015).

"The Vestige" was first published in *Nowhereville: Weird Is Other People*, edited by Scott Gable and C. Dombrowski (Broken Eye Books, 2019).

"The Unknown Chambers" was first published in *Gothic Lovecraft*, edited by Lynne Jamneck and S. T. Joshi (Cycatrix Press, 2016).

"So Much Wine" was first published in *Supernatural Tales* #42 (Winter 2019/20), edited by David Longhorn.

"An Element of Blank" was first published in *Supernatural Tales* #30 (Autumn 2015), edited by David Longhorn.

"The Seventh Wave" was first published in *Terror Tales of the Ocean*, edited by Paul Finch (Gray Friar Press, 2015).

"Knots" is published here for the first time.

# Acknowledgements

Writing never happens in a vacuum, and no writer creates without being indebted to many, many people—far more than could ever be acknowledged. Foremost among those I must thank, however, are the editors who first published these stories: Simon Strantzas, Peter Coleborn and Pauline E. Dungate, Mark Beech, Scott Gable and C. Dombrowski, Lynne Jamneck and S. T. Joshi, David Longhorn, and Paul Finch. Thanks go as well to Simon Strantzas and Stephen Jones for choosing "The Seventh Wave" for year's best anthologies. Andy Cox, Michael Kelly, and Stephen Jones have all been there for me at so many pivotal points in my career, helping and encouraging me by believing in my writing and just in so many more ways that I can enumerate or that they'll ever know.

Then there are the many writers with whom I share this strange pastime, and with whom I've had intense or passing conversations online or in real life, a drink, a laugh, a long afternoon, or night at the pub (you know who you are), but particular thanks must go to three especially stalwart recipients of my angst and sources of encouragement and pep talks: Steve Duffy, Maura McHugh, and Simon Bestwick. Sean Hogan, my first reader, never stops believing in me even when I don't believe in myself. Thanks go to James Bacon for his unflagging enthusiasm, support and practical help.

The physical book that you're holding would not be what it is without the efforts of Steve J. Shaw, Meggan Kehrli,

John Coulthart, Timothy J. Jarvis, and Jim Rockhill. Rob Shearman is a dear friend as well as a terrific writer who took time out of his busy schedule to pen an introduction for me. And of course, Brian J. Showers was infinitely patient with my many delays as he shepherded this book through the publication process with all the exquisite care that he gives to every book released by Swan River Press.

Most of all, thanks to you, the reader, for joining me here and letting me tell you some stories. It's you I write for, to connect across the distance of space and time and to find a common humanity in the boundlessness of imagination, even when we meet in the dark.

# About the Author

Lynda E. Rucker has written more than fifty stories for various magazines and anthologies. She contributed a segment to *The Ghost Train Doesn't Stop Here Anymore*, an anthology of horror plays produced on London's West End, won the Shirley Jackson Award for Best Short Story in 2015, and edited *Uncertainties III* for Swan River Press. Her previous collections include *The Moon Will Look Strange* and *You'll Know When You Get There*.

# SWAN RIVER PRESS

Founded in 2003, Swan River Press is an independent
publishing company, based in Dublin, Ireland, dedicated
to gothic, supernatural, and fantastic literature. We special-
ise in limited edition hardbacks, publishing fiction from
around the world with an emphasis on Ireland's contribu-
tions to the genre.

www.swanriverpress.ie

*"While small publishers often produce beautiful books,
few can match those from Swan River Press."*

– Washington Post

*"It [is] often down to small, independent, specialist presses
to keep the candle of horror fiction flickering . . . "*

– The Irish Times

*"Swan River Press—cutting edge of New Gothic."*

– Joyce Carol Oates

*"The redoubtable Brian J. Showers [keeps] the
myriad voices of Irish fantasy alive there in Dublin."*

– Alan Moore

# YOU'LL KNOW WHEN YOU GET THERE

Lynda E. Rucker

A woman returns home to revisit an encounter with the numinous; couples take up residence in houses full of sinister secrets; a man fleeing a failed marriage discovers something ancient and unknowable in rural Ireland . . .

In her introduction, Lisa Tuttle observes that "certain places are doomed, dangerous in some inexplicable, metaphysical way", and the characters in these stories all seem drawn in their own ways to just such places, whether trying to return home or endeavouring to get as far from life as possible. These nine stories by Shirley Jackson Award winner Lynda E. Rucker tell tales of those lost and searching, often for something they cannot name, and encountering along the way the uncanny embedded in the everyday world.

*"Indirection is a special skill and it's one that Lynda E. Rucker uses frequently to emphasise those near indefinable moments of social alienation and paranoia, that you just want to get up and run far, far away from."*

– Adam L. G. Nevill

*"Lynda is the genuine article—a serious, literary author of 'quiet horror' whose work is disquieting, inspiring, and oddly reassuring. It's good to know that there are writers so gifted working in our genre."*

– *Supernatural Tales*

# HERE WITH
# THE SHADOWS

Steve Rasnic Tem

*"Far better to choose an absence
than to have an absence forced upon you."*

These stories by award-winning author Steve Rasnic Tem
drag from the darkness ghosts that haunt us all. Between
these covers lurk the spectres of grief, loss, and loneliness:
a man discovers he is far from alone in his empty home, a
forlorn wife is gifted with an unusual child, a contractor
contemplates the sad message left by a grieving father, a
blind woman discovers a spiritual manifestation at the
edge of a forest, a spectral presence appears in a lonesome
Colorado wheat field . . . *Here with the Shadows* is a
volume of supernatural impressions and quiet vacancies,
and in each story Tem reminds us that sometimes only a
whisper separates us from the eternal.

*"Perfect gems of storytelling whose impact
is like that of poetry."*

– Locus

*"Loneliness is next to ghostliness, and the isolation and sorrow
of the bereaved play a role in luring revenants to the door."*

– Totally Dublin

*"These little literary soupçon's are must-reads."*

– Weird Fiction Review

# TREATISES ON DUST

Timothy J. Jarvis

*"From the small bones of the middle ear
can be fashioned a key."*

"For a while now," Timothy J. Jarvis tells us in the first tale
here, "I've been collecting texts that hint at strange tales."
He goes on to explain that these "Treatises on Dust" are
not ghost stories in the traditional sense. Indeed none of
the pieces in the collection could be said to be in the vein
of traditional supernatural fiction. They are haunted, not
by ghosts, but by an obscure volume of French decadent
poetry, a seventeenth-century murder ballad, a bone
antenna, and by places where "the membrane is thin".

They cleave closer to what the literary hermit of
Arthur Machen's *Hieroglyphics* called "ecstasy". Though
perhaps an ecstasy found less in the "withdrawal from the
common life and the common consciousness", than one
grubbed up from the murk of that very consciousness.

*"There is plenty to entertain lovers of weird fiction."*

– Supernatural Tales